Monologue for a Shipwreck

George Schaub

1_____

On my fog bound coast there is no Turner sky. The light that shines down on us all is diffused and there is no way to judge the direction of its source. No time from the angle of the blessed rays can be told and all watches are still. The time told is only from when the clocks ran down, a lack of batteries causing the inconvenience. Or when the face met a more dramatic end cracked by fall or rage. No time is a wall of mist and reality a carrot dangled before a mule. Out of the mist something occasionally emerges but I'm not sure what it is. Even when it approaches closer I'm uncertain of it because I do not know its origins or motives. The threat is veiled but isn't it always.

Sharing these musings and doubts does little good, as everyone has retreated to their cave and there's no one here who will dispute or agree. The motivation around here is survival and

accumulation and how much
accumulation depends on how much
accumulation you think you need to
survive. It's difficult to keep track of
who belongs to what, or what belongs
to whom. This mist makes it difficult
to ascertain boundaries. Perhaps we
need alarms to sound should anything
be disturbed, a plausible solution to the
constant problem of keeping track of
things under these conditions. But if
the borders are close and the mists
heavy then the noise could emanate
from any possible pile and not
necessarily from one's own. Of course
the pile could be alarmed with a
personal noise or even smell so that
whenever one's own pile is molested
then the disturbance will be evident
and something could be done about the
violation. What that action might be is
hard to imagine because the actual
cause of the disturbance would be
difficult to know and if it's a force
greater than one's self or some natural
occurrence (whatever that might mean)
then it would probably be wiser to do

nothing or better to retreat (where?) so that the pile would be sacrificed for the sake of one's skin. Better to lose the pile and live to accumulate another day. You might think that this endless cycle of avarice and cowardice is a less than noble way to exist but it's the way things are done around here and who am I to buck the trend?

The mists from this edge of land and sea blow on a ceaseless wind. There is rarely any diminution of its opacity and forces continually conspire towards its manufacture. There seems to be a funnel into which a certain temperature and moisture commingle and out the tapered end where we sit it exhales endlessly. Whatever topography there is I've forgotten and there's nothing much to remind me about what might have been. Geology lessons have been wasted on me. The light varies slightly. Of course there is day and night and a fading of day to night and a glimmering at dawn. We're not in a total void there is some reality this is not metaphysical prose. We convince ourselves that we occupy some corner of the earth and that we seek to elucidate our position but it usually leads us into a spiral of faulty logic ending us in the place where we become our own grandfather, regardless of gender or inclination, drowning in his own blood in some trench in western France nearly a century ago, or so they told me.

Something flies by my ear occasionally and I'm unsure if it's a bullet or a bird. I sense the wind but only in the way it makes me feel warmer or colder depending on the season and latitude. There is some tenuous connection with it all despite how alienated or alone I might feel or be. There may be a hum somewhere perhaps a wire overhead a distant motor or some insect honing in for a drink. There may even be a flurry of activity beyond the veil in front of my eyes. I can only hope it is receding but curiosity still quickens my heart but it's better not to move perhaps there is a precipice just beyond the mist and that flurry ended quickly, didn't it?

So let's not move let's not change let's not be too abrupt in our motion. Let's you and I just sit it out for a while together and negotiate some truce so we don't end up killing each other. I have no inclination to do you any harm and I'm feeling talkative. I don't expect any particular reaction but an occasional nod would be nice and I promise to recognize and affirm your presence by continuing to talk because talking to myself brings me in circles and getting there is half the fun. So I'll tell you a story and it's about this place and what we do here. Perhaps the stories will bring back memories or serve as cautionary tales to the uninitiated. Perhaps it will make you yearn for the mists to dissipate to reveal all, though I doubt that, or will hypnotize you further into alienation where you feel eminently more comfortable and at home anyway.

2_____

It begins with a small poem, if you
will.

"Dental florists numbing
somnambulists
All fallen on novocaine
Foster home of the blind
Where is your airline stewardess
Peaceful now?"

Who will guide us here? Virgil,
Beatrice or Dante who once guided
was content to write the tour book?

What follows describes events that
could only be intuited, as all that took
place could not be seen. Cause, effect
and chaos happen simultaneously,
which means that one thing you should
learn is when to duck. It may all be a
projection from the mind to the misty
screen but the mind has to get it from
somewhere and the experience has to
be shared to be real so the grammar,
shaky at best, should unfold a

sequence of people and events to tell the tale.

And a tale is what it is, beginning like all good yarns with the thinnest excuse of a calamity then redemption then some moral lesson learned and goodnight. This blip on the screen is noted in passing in the rush of events hardly a distraction for those seeking cleaner sinks and gas-free après-dining experiences.

And so it begins here again on this fog bound coast where a ship whose masts chimed like crystal chandeliers when the windows are thrown open in a Victorian novel was battered rudderless in treacherous waters inside the five-mile limit no gambling boats allowed only on the deck where the moon glinted off sullen eyes too long forgotten.

On what specific coast you may well ask. It's the land where the flesh divinities sacrifice the rental obituaries for a month in the frozen wastes, a tundra of solitary confinees who never quite made the grade. They set up shop in crumbling walls their feelers stabbing the air in cockroach anticipation clamoring for a piece of the action. Their goods the castoffs of tertiary markets returned and re-boxed with indifference or the washed-off remnants of three day old dumpster vegetables, if you cook it long enough it makes a tolerable stew. If these are the goods imagine the sellers. Now imagine the buyers and then conjure up those to whom they bring this merchandise home in some mediocre triumph then visualize those homes and the streets on which they are scattered the shattered billboards made jagged from the cruel wind. That's where we be.

Being one such native I glanced sideways through infrared eye and noticed the ship becoming shards on this simmering volcanic shore. I made my way through the glowering

crevasses where the mist, now pushed
by a kinder almost casual wind, flowed
through holes formed by bubbling
rocks millions of years ago, perhaps
made larger by fervent fingernails
ripping away at the edges attempting
to stave off hunger and suffocation,
then collapse. To elucidate, the danger
here is lack of oxygen the failure to be
able to see from the valley to the
mountains on even the clearest day.
This should tell the occupants that
harder days are to come and that
perhaps moving would be a wiser
course, but they rarely do.

As I go I pass the usual stiffs and
beggars the washouts the blank stares
every day in the same alcove they can't
seem to venture ten feet beyond their
own personal station of the cross,
where they plant a flag in the hopes of
a salutation but it's best, I can assure
you, to avert your glance from their
festering maladies which they hold
aloft, the better to see you my dear, as
it only encourages them and others

who seem to benefit from their
guidance and it only means more of
them in your path what a drag it's hard
enough to get around these days
anyway. So avoid this unseemly
display and be aware of the
divisiveness of birth on that very day
we become separated from the great
void and spend our time staring out to
sea getting a tan wondering why we
left in the first place. What price
compassion? It's like pouring water
into a bottomless well these black
holes suck in energy and precious
time. They spin yarns like webs and
entangle you in puzzles no one can
solve and even if solved have no point
except taking up your time. Step over
or step aside but keep on your noble
way without a thought on their
pleasure or pain and don't be provoked
and don't be diverted from your
conquering fate and quest for ever
higher modes of self-involvement.

Now the sky is washed in sullen
pastels and we begin to turn over

pocked rocks in the hopes of finding
an unsuspected meal. The usual
flittering crabs and oil-soaked seaweed
don't you think it's sad when you're
reduced to eating scavengers and
detritus, no matter how fancy the
sauce? There can be no payment that
would ameliorate this devastation.
Perhaps this shipwreck will toss ashore
some tidbit on this surly tide. For now
we must bite deep into our hands in
anticipation to stave off the pain and
watch as the heat of the day causes the
tidal pools to steam. A coarse starfish,
inedible even in the direst
circumstances moves like the hands of
a clock toward some stranded mollusk,
just as I pick my way towards the
rough planks that slosh brutally against
the coarse shore.

I see a survivor clutching desperately
to some torn flotsam, the oily water
forcing his eyelids closed and causing
blood to drip from nose and ears
surrounded by jellyfish that sting for

the fun of it and bring blood up
through the pores of his skin.

Okay, we're going to try for some
empathy here, some compassion some
putting ourselves in his shoes, if he
had them. Sensations lost from the
neck down and numbness a welcome
relief after unendurable pain vomiting
up the salty brine through nose and
mouth swirling in a whirlpool staring
sightless wondering when the center
will suck you down to the crab's
gleeful surprise. Losing logic in an
eruption of despair as bubbles race
through the spinal column up to the
frantic cerebrum, all functions swirling
in a timeless vision of death and
linkages snapped open pouring forth
this jumbled flow:

arrows green flashing—missed
directions through ornate tunnel crystal
synapse snapping thinking you're
driving vertically rather than the
expected straight ahead, glad handing
the regal tomb after the admission

price had been paid, expectations of
some pomp under the circumstances
but just another tick on the clicker--
meditations of the million silent ones
raising their shaven heads in unison
glistening in the bare sun winking the
one big eye flowing robes in the desert
summer rain it never touches the
ground--incandescent black and white
strobes flash alternately one projecting
all the others absorbing all there is no
gray no in between no space or time
for reflection only geometric intricacy
that breaks the line into a million
permutations of form--a crooked finger
beckons toward another plane where
all the glowing shapes meet in the orb
where parallel lines come to rest and
get acquainted, where molten triangles
become brilliant specters and pulse in
the rhythm of diminishing heartbeats,
traveling through space with open
arms and outspread palms unlocking
the heat of vanquished stars that died a
billion years ago but still throw out
images of lives long lost, a flash in the
midsummer night you mistake for

some comet or a firefly until death
rises cold and bold from down under
and opens its arms for the last embrace
and invites the melting mind to flow in
some greater stream--there is no
fleeing over terrain spinning like a top
hills and valleys a mere pace in dream
boots because death looking typical is
gliding in velvet robes on the current
of bats fleeing their steeple nests for
the midnight feast there is no reason to
flee it only forestalls the fear so turn
and meet the kiss and the enfolding
arms

There follows, I am assured, some
silence.

Some emptiness of space, a shrug of
time as it meets itself at the helix
crossroads. Inhale and exhale deeply
ten times, slow now. Make your
shuttering breaths of eternal wait.
From the ground in which you were
swallowed will come a murmur of
quiet desire. The wish may be of
remembrance or the illusion that things

will be better the second time around.
It seems unlikely but that yearning is
enough to earn another ride on the
merry-go-round.

Why come back you may well ask?

There may be a longing for the soft
blue light of morning, for the sound of
rain on a tin roof, for the embrace of a
warm and laughing companion, for the
touch of moss on bare feet, for the
sweetness of air in autumn's first
arrival, for the coolness of water and
its shimmering blue, for the woven
snow in the forest for the sound of a
million voices in the stream the basso
continuo of the surf on a palm-lined
shore the quiet turn of the deer's
attentive head and all conscious
thoughts wondered at in silence for the
hand of a child reaching toward yours
for the cadence of music strength in
the lifting arm the clearness of vision
after the wind has swept the valley
clear the eye's delight in the rainbow
and the shadow as it contorts form.

These quiet desires cause a shoot to tentatively break the ground and from that sprig a plant grows and stretches its branches and leaves strong and tall toward the nurturing sun. Color forms to nourish the weary eye. As the wind spreads your seeds for others to enjoy you relinquish thoughts of death and await the endurance contest to follow. So die, or deny death and be washed onto this merciless shore and await the sounds and heed these observations.

3

Mine is not the only sentient being cruising these shores. Other heads ease from behind the ripped rocks to reveal their scarred foreheads and squinting eyes. These veterans in the combat of survival also peruse the mass of wood and flesh arranging itself on the beach in splintered confusion. They see the hand grasping toward the sky and those nostrils gushing snot and oil and observe those deep holes of black where eyes once stared, limbs torn and battered from the merciless meeting of sea and shore. They all can appreciate how rare a sight it is for one to reach our shores. But they also see the other scavengers and note how they have gathered ready to claim this lucky find. I have neither special claim to make nor particular strength nor charm nor weapon that would have the others yield this find, but this being my projection onto the mist that tells this tale and the fact that I'm not prepared to yield to another narrator who would in essence be another projection of myself and taking you into consideration and knowing that there is little sense in causing an interruption in what to this point has been a fairly smooth digression and hopefully diversion I will approach the sprawled form and engage it in the matters to follow, only to avoid confusion you understand.

Of course out of the habit of survival I take two steps forward and one back as I go scattering the thickening mists of my awareness as any approach to another form has a tendency to cause one to do. I finally reach the spot of my curiosity and desire and squat to better inspect the prey, no--object of my compassion--and prod it with a splinter of wood from the smashed plank it clutched and address the being most courteously:

"Ah, and welcome to this most commodious abode pardon the festering wind but it comes with the season the tourist board wishes to assure all visitors that this passing inconvenience is being overseen by a minor god of the last occupants who, thinking that his acolytes still inhabit the area creates occasional havoc due to the lack of oblations and sacrifices of course the feast days are still observed hollow affairs actually but what were we to do with all those ornate chalices and costumes? Forgive the lack of formal obligatory haughty nonsense but I lack the degrees to address you prosperously my heathen ways upset you in the least I take it my disadvantaged, dismembered sullen shipwreck for as far as you can see you have landed on that famed postcard isle and I am the king dressed in resplendent robes, what with your eyes the sorry mass of jelly they be no doubt hors d'oeuvres for some cruising crab."

I adjusted my stance. "But have no fear for I shall guide you through our curious world, glowing accounts, the latest reports from the front, the images coming while I brush my teeth. You might prefer a direct download but then you'd be me and you wouldn't want that and with all due respect the feeling is mutual even though every message we receive and morsel we stuff in our mouth is intended to make us all one it's really a matter of control who wants to deal with so many individuals but for the life of me I can't figure out why they should act that way it's often just a bother to get out of bed."

He stirred. "No, speak not, no need to explain there will be no excuses offered and no apologies accepted or expected we're nothing here if not polite and take kindness as the best approach and only path to follow. So let me drag you to the putrid pit in this swollen fragment of earth I call home and there delight your expectant ears with tales of our land and the princes and consorts who occupy it and with every breath exude a fragrance that blesses each soul that dances in the wind of an ever-fraying demeanor. To what end? Why to better equip you when you recover so that you can go begging on our tenuous highways and be beaten and scorned for every crumb you stuff in your grumbling belly. I only have your welfare at heart."

4_____

A distant thunder startles the vultures that cast themselves from precipitous branches into vectors that help them glide along the valley wall. Their wings are fixed at a certain angle and they merely flex to change direction or raise or lower their height of flight. This would seem like an effortless way to travel. Petitioners to the court lack this ease of transportation and must rely on those who reside in the back estuaries to pole their craft through murky swamps to visit the golden cities where all mingle minds. Their panchromatic naiveté, their sartorial neglect their despondent demeanor make them early birds seeking the slide sensation. While shadows of arithmetic hawks inscribe parabolic

palavers on the striated canyon walls
these warrants of the court hunt
poisoned pigeons while loitering on
park benches awaiting any sun to
shine.

Above the fray green castles, hung
with Masonic tapestries, serve as home
to laconic minions who make it their
life's work to escape the chaining
room. Loitering executioners on
cigarette breaks hang out on the moat's
left bank, posing passive questions
about marked men who brag they were
once the cornerstones of the empire's
overextended vaults. The queen is
resting with the lancer while bleak
plagiarizers stalk the ribald head of the
crown prince. His ravings have
become increasingly inaccurate and he
labels any hi-jinx as heretical. He
defies the serfs to bloat themselves at
the annual feast of the eighteen
martyred dwarfs. Would he have them
fast?

The nights were a daze when moonless cracks appeared in the starlit sky, meteoric calculations by corrupt astronomers foretold of the big mix-up. Even the monks managed to mangle their masochistic manuscripts and mortgaged millennium mileage. They wanted to impose temple surcharges for the sacrificial lamb, but the boys with the battering ram soon deserted, not even switching sides but heading for any bodily border they could ascertain. That didn't last long. We hear the rats are now genuflecting for snotty gargoyles taking the cross town bus to the elimination zone.

The least of them sat in the rubble surveying the accomplishments of the scientific age. The scarred planet still spins but the air is befouled with their belching. They took a balanced equation and turned it on its head. They wore tinted glasses and made deals with the rabid bat, synthesizing mysteries and creating spirits before their time. They took Sunday's last supper and strung the apostles like puppets on some decorative whirl, but soon decided there was no room at the inn for Armageddon's horseless riders. After the rationalists cleaned their hands of blood the poperish pugilists rushed in and drenched the land once more with their semi-financial dubious return operations, hoping for that last chance oasis and the opportunity to drift with the ground water through limestone caves into their battalion's helium control complex. Uranium studded bottle stoppers coagulated along with the agent orange, causing frosted pains supposedly relieved by a visit from the prelate himself blessing the ammunition with a jigger of snot, his grizzled visage blurry eyed but still holding on, his left hand with the shakes but the right holding the collaborator's bible as steady as a rock hound in a petrified forest.

(The locket lay on the nape of her neck where the vein softly pounded his eyes closed on her on that place where the

hair touched her shoulder his eyes
opened a bead of sweat traveled slowly
down the edge of her brow.)

The last platoon fell in briefly with
some cases of unicorn flesh and
fortunately for all concerned left the
premises with only a minor bust up
and precious furniture overtures, their
calloused hands obstinate, yet later
pleading for lesser charges. Heroes
abounded but were often hounded with
nagging doubts about internal bouts
under the gray sky discordant helix
counterpoints. The nadir peaked
mountainous trespasses, an elemental
shift in the bilingual possibilities. They
all spoke the same wheel but never
mangled to communicate.

The bridge and surrounding piazza is
still pockmarked with bullets fifty
years later the pleasant row of trees
along the promenade at the edge of
town is where they hung the partisans.
Now the valley sweeps away and those
who wept then have joined the

sacrifice but lovers always mention it
on their tour. As their eyes pause over
the site they scan the walk where at
night small lights mark where each of
them dangled.

(The room was unrelieved red the
tapestry hung over the lamp to blunt
the glare.)

Heathen grape vines pollute the holy
water with thoughts of conjugal bliss.
Under moth eaten pup tents they sleep
while Mardi Gras passes into Lent, the
orb with no tentacles aloft on a parking
meter feeling a slight breeze as the
celebrants sweep past, bearing the
singular sensation of the slow death
spiral, watching the turning of the
pages of a book read backwards, a
series of pictures with no particular
rhyme, then the circle closes and it's
end of story but the time locks always
have room for one more, even steven
balancing the hopeless books,
outlasting the temptation to rummage
in the garbage for the final solution,

viewing portraits painted on shattered glass, aren't you astounded by the likeness?

After the results were in Goliath demanded a rematch, we all regret the left when we should have gone right, the smile rather than the grimace or the frown but those great expectations may be unwarranted by ego extensions of our sympathies, those nervous nellies in the pit of the butterfly's stomach, pausing on the back seat waiting for the rise the flashlight barks and its off to the races. Those were tender times but those burly heavyweight theatrics gave everyone stage fright perhaps the next arrow in the air will find its mark where did you learn such behavior? Of course the parents but I mean before then and before then from where does that instinct stem? Tough deal, but all the actors have gone home and the audience is sleeping it off in the tombs.

You can scream and hold your breath for as long as it takes but perhaps you

might consider loosening your spare
time and taking a dry spell. The
courtyard is piled with garbage mostly
crumbled paper where cats prowl and
fly from windows tossed by derelicts
who do nothing but lift weights and
hang out waiting for large cars and
people to pull in from across the river,
where they sprawl in the candy
wrappers and red bricks the dresser
drawers filled with used bills few of
them in greater denominations than
one.

The information booth is circled by
forty bespectacled lawyers and sage
and dust blew against the bail bond
signs on the forsaken highway.
Counsels in black armbands are
soliciting your case, the ping-pong ball
is stolen from your snorkel, the
periscope is looking backwards the
mast is torn and we are adrift. Are
those breakers I hear? Surely not a
good sound when land is supposed to
be so far away.

We were scouring the bathtub sea
looking for hospital ships to torpedo.
Outside it's a hundred degrees and
ninety eight percent humidity, the
smoke hanging low and mean and
there's no way to get out of here fast
enough but we're laden down with
cloth from the tundra, just having
arrived off the grand tour where the
natives gave us nothing but hard looks.
We got back to find the hot water
turned off and the locks all changed so
we bust the doors and run down the
fire escape just another escapade but
that's what you get for carousing with
the enemy rusted metal and scraped
hands each step like a telephone
slammed on the hook. They have more
tenderness for their dogs. Our leaders
scrambled through the alleys their herd
bloodied and sprawled among last
night's edition, the controllers
salivating through their rotten guns,
making tents out of our bed sheets and
getting ready for the ultimate test.
Eager ears waited on the edge of the
desert as scholars ridiculed covenants

of love in the parlors of a more
delicate breed.

(There is a line forming but nothing
but bored looks when you've seen it all
before, but there is always a surprise
package awaiting an opening.)

5 _____

To be sure there were moments of glory shrouded in the modernity, just another point of view, even the angels were on the take. The emulations cast aspersions on the patron, but on the surface nothing but smiles. Clustered on street corners, they were harassed by manic cops, the arches shrouded with bougainvillea the mirrors clouded with ash from a distant volcano that murmurs through the night, on plazas where Christmas lights stay festooned the entire year, it being hot always so who could tell just what season it might be. It lights the beggars in delightful colors, poor people in colorful clothes just another subject for a snap. The tour bus leaves them in the dust with hollow promises of magazine covers and the face pressed against the glass in that classic pose, the heat and dust clogging pores as sullen midnight tiptoes around dawn's corner, bashful and aghast under the blinking blue light, inside the scuffed linoleum the only sign of the brawl, rain having washed away the remnants of whatever riot was unrecorded by the official press.

Only the fetid tide washes on theses shores, not really caring about the moon, a slight differential between high and low, a brief wave against the pilings of the exclusive estates that have laid claim to these bits of sand.

There were promises made, some kept with delicate glances from hard eyes, hoping to exit promptly when the signals change, though there's a tendency to wave at whatever passes. Armature figures stretch to their limits, empty hands wooden with desire, one tortured twin claiming to be the better half with desperate Siamese looking for a connection. Form and color blur, the quiet eye condescends to perceive, right angles forming with protractor precision and reflections all aglow about the trisection and how it drove the math lads mad. When mirror met mirror there was nothing but repeating form, the viewer hard pressed to know when the image begins being a being and when reality ends. It's finding the space in space that seems to cause the most difficulty, especially when the rent's so high. There's always the four-wall solution, and the hammer, the nail and glass to create those borders. But space travel is futile we are already in space.

The last contact was cut along with the silver thread, centrifugal force finally failed and the synapse synopsis split for the coast, gone tilt so the summation was truncated by the shards of humanity that sat splintered and bewildered by that last fall. Swept away by the beatification of the semi-holy, and the constant drone of the olfactory nerve, the deafening quiet, the sixty cycle buzz, it was enough to send the priests scurrying to the confessionals, where grids diffracted the light shining through their leery eyes. The doorway squat the inevitable coffee cup the pants too loose the upward squint the inevitable refusal.

The turf was divided into fifteen zones, all neatly bordered by some thorny shrub where even careful sparrows were impaled, the needles washing up on this chaotic shore. As smile fades to grimace, so quickly, you notice, if you keep your eye on the gathering, the face tilts toward hands that seek a tattered cloth to touch. Or was it eyes looking upward that tell the tale, a forgotten myth that makes the DNA crawl? The evolution from particle to wave causes some how shall I say gentle lapping on the shore at least enough tidal flow to awaken the crabs.

That hat is pulled way too low so the next step better be intuitive, the papers are properly shuffled and the words rearranged, making a garbled past palatable, those theories that only yesterday made so much sense. Any attempt to codify the information is rightfully met with scorn, as pettiness eliminated any hope of reconciliation. The momentary bow is preceded by another mix-up, a compromise with alien spirits being an option. But time ill spent is never repaid by a universe with no tomorrow. The tangle of noise cancels out any conversation with those attempting to set a course, especially when the disenfranchisement has become so rampant, a mentality that always whistles in the dark. Fear can tremble even the stiffest upper lip when nasty revelations arrive at dawn.

There could be no restoration of that crumbling wall where paint attempts to wash over the years, for any installation can only be perceived by those who condemn this harsh treaty. There can be no compromise here, the alternative being the beating of wings as the crows make their retreat from passion subdivided, no matter how much amusement one might derive from contemplating the mess.

6_____

So much for the operational code.
When the spirit moves the flesh is
weak, making bargains with tentative
deities just in case, and it does
manifest itself in the strangest ways,
facial expressions akimbo, the eye a
meaningful twitch, each lobe tuned to
different frequencies, like the static
border between radio stations on that
midnight drive, the hockey game
intermixed with the mine disaster, and
who's keeping score? Moving two
miles down the road and there's that
trailer plastered with images from the
last solar flare, a celestial mix-up when
calendars clashed and the fragrant
culture was run out of town. There was
no justification for that odd behavior,
rectifying past sins with a bang on the
drum, today's revelation being paying
for the penance on the installment
plan.

Can we again attain that lofty
perspective, where we can scratch our
heads and rub our hands in the crystal

room, the light all dazzling and the Chinese barmaid such a twit, to retreat to that aluminum enclosure and count the take, that rented wreck surrounded by alabaster trees and the false bravado where bare lights surrounded by ersatz quartz crystals dare to foretell the future? The terrible depot closed down on account of the phase of the moon the whole circus coming down like a lead balloon, drifting journeys on a stream too red from the slag, the bubbles a thousand tongues now strangled by the prospect of drinking such vile liquid, mumbling the three kings' names and struggling to remember what gifts they had brought.

The degradation charts are maligned up on distant wall, a most precise polyphony punctuates the pugilistic program in the lost hope that lassitude and the ugly spike will cause a cathartic capitulation among those ordering stasis as the lunch special for today. Functionaries ignorant of their function gather at the junction and title

filmstrips for the sensational crew, a
fast break toward cashing out when the
last ferry just left for the estuary.
Those street crossing denials, those
attitudinal shifts, noting the raising of
an eyebrow with infinite caress,
folding of hands with index finger
bent, it's some kind of blessing, right?
Or is it just because the sculptor
couldn't quite get it right? That's how
these myths get rolling, that critical
angle, that gang sign no one quite gets
and directions everyone forgets to get
out of the sprawl. Lobby fanatics
browse bellicose intentions for clues to
creating an elastic and molded
personality borrowed from some pulp
fiction novel the author having no idea
about anything but paying the rent but
later is taken as gospel and lives are
won and lost and roads traveled
because of some obscure phrase
striking the lost souls as the way, the
Tao, the true intention of their spirit.
The true end some forlorn alley some
three-day-old stew some wrong
intention even the slightest sense of

self interest would have long ago
defined all that as decidedly being not
the road to travel.

As in, the engineer of flesh trains
making the final commutation run in
dense crowded eye lacerations, the fog
again shrouding this shore, all the
faces a million eyes all pushed into
one, the space getting tighter, forced to
stand in puddles of dubious origin, the
only room in acidic crunch of thorny
entities. A billion thought patterns
aligned no mean feat but hey that's
what TV is for to send all to dull
staring at the filthy floor no eye
contact because then we might get the
bright idea that there's something to
talk about other than shifting weight in
a most contraposto way, screeching
wheels metal against metal drill gaping
holes in the mind's eye, oxygen
content approaching zero, our local
maniac having chosen this precise time
to coordinate his four thousand years
of rage with your very presence, the
utter ugliness, the dark, flickering

moments, the grasping hands the trembling flesh, the sound of brief and sudden inhalation, the shuffling feet, the force of survival clawed by inevitable despair. Above ground, investment bankers in stretch limos scan the rates on loans calculated to raise the interest on smothering misery. Perhaps a simplification like those Russian Constructivist Bolsheviks but you can't help but admire the graphics.

Priorities here are consummated by total machinations paid off in kind remembrances of the fatal stare the accident emerging from the inevitable syndrome, amorphous clouds forming in the western sky, there's no denying we're in for some strange brew. Only the long gone sage could have foretold this, but he packed his bags along with the Delphic Oracle and beat a hasty retreat on the last bus down that dusty road. The corn fields, the manmade lake, the trailers sizzling in the summer sun, the deep sigh, the bright light careening past the corner of the nomad's tent. The integers have long been abandoned on muddy beaches along with their dripping sensibilities, harlot predators hawking cure-alls on the twisted avenues of dissent, equality squabbles precluded by the push of the button.

All those authoritarian convivialities have been sent reeling like a kite in a hurricane tethered to the boardwalk where splinters greeted the drinkers whose tattoos proclaimed some incestuous brand, the masks slipping from loosened knots revealing the basic child cringing under the covers in fear of the partially open closet door. That spider sits patiently in the web, those gills breathe slowly in expectant swamps, that programmed robot giving predictable and classic responses to confused artifacts, marching them out of the big room without even a sentimental goodbye. Or they wave and weep and then turn away and wonder hey what's for lunch. The undulating breath of a negligent universe offers no massages for the weary mind, such misdemeanor tragedies causing us to pause on the precipice to consider harmless entreaties to our deaf gods, our prayers echoing back, empty, in mocking innocence.

The necklace of satellites the space junk the transmission beams the telemetry the foil wrapped crap the wanton technology all send casual reports to a world strung out on a silver thread, a universe filled with misnomers and gremlins with golden scissors. There's one gentle snip that will change the game, evolution-wise, so to speak, and any delicate sense of reality will go slipping down the continuum, sweeping away forlorn mystics who already gave up the ghost, who packed their crystal balls and headed for the hills.

The act long played out the pretenders left bleak in a Sumerian outhouse, the

old truck the tires slashed the
windshield smashed the stuffing from
the seats gone and just the springs
remain, hardly decent rest for the
wandering minstrel on the midnight
highway, looking for a break from the
wind, no moon, just the pebbles
careening into the ditch a guide. The
other side of the coin sits cross town
where dharma cyclists are hung up on
the wheel, they keep spinning the same
old tale but hey who wants to leave
this bliss, raised hands in hope seeking
warmth from the noonday sun, brief
encounters in green tile plazas, off into
space ships to tour the planets, holding
on through the winter of weeks, buds
may again bloom have hope, there is a
more compassionate hand to play.

7_____

Soft footsteps trace the dusty parade
grounds, a sideways glance reveals a
weeper under the bleachers, crying for
the ghost of victory, the grand game,
the lethal surcharge deafening the
bursting dawn, smoke on the horizon
they've set the wells ablaze, the plain
tilted, an unsteady gait, a carefully
choreographed shrug all being placed
in mosaic remembrances.

Sleeping it off in the pews with the
bishop who always felt rooked,
chewing my ear off about the blonde in
the third row and the latest stuff the
local talent the cool breezes in that
tropical village, shotguns propped up
against the chili parlor wall, dim light
protruding through the empty hall, a
painting hung askew covering the
inevitable crack, evidence of the last
earthen rumble that passed through
town, less paint than rubbed in dust
and sweat, I so wanted to phone out
but lacked the coin then in circulation
and the sheer will to dial. Waiting for

the bus the chickens scratch the
cobblestones it never comes and
people look at me like I'm an idiot
wondering why is he standing at the
bus stop when the bus never comes?

You see a table that rocks with every
stroke of the pen the barkeep eyeing
me wondering how long can he nurse
that drink the coffee cup rim marred
with cheap lipstick the dishwasher
failed to catch or perhaps a private
balcony overlooking the courtyard
filled with flowers the rooftops stretch
out wash the vaunted breeze drying the
sheets the soft dust from the street
rising the plaintive cry of a child the
laughter of women the beaded curtain
parts and a tray with ice and citrus
leads the way and behind comes a
hand delicate offering the eyes a
golden glow. But some harlequin bigot
cuts in on the line tapping his empty
bowl with a shattered spoon,
carbonized and defensive causing
actions that stir the whiplash neck the
consumption of hideous feasts the

earthbound sanctity forcing a
semblance of lamentation, holding a
wilting flower in the screaming rain,
praying for that memory of a rooftop
and a warm hand, all a clear case of a
tenuous arrangement with some
hopeless deity.

Insensitive notables plod makeshift in
no decision contests, incurable
vampires cruise eighth avenue's
midnight corridors where infinity
conspires with figure eight neon to
create a somnambulistic view that
seeks eternal bliss in four minute
showdowns, the cards have it or they
don't, the bet runner kicking over the
plate of chicken, the shouts dwindle as
the chips run down, the mocking house
taking ever greater rakes on each hand,
not to worry if you got nothing in the
hole only bluffers claim their filled
hand that early in the game. That pale
green fluorescent suit, those baggy
knees, those frayed cuffs make it hard
to turn on the cool, leaving bottomless
pits in the potted palm of a trembling

hand, a free ride around the corner to a blood bank where you can cash in on your own type.

The parables were stalled, etched in shifting sands, washed away by the rising tide, like gem sparkled gown drifting past the cosmic kiosk where auto smashups light the gray lads selling tokens to the flesh barns, acrobatics and the gleeful smiles of the ladies of the orange sky.

8_____

These are of course arbitrary
admissions, bereft of administrative
awkwardness, not bashful by a long
run but sullen nonetheless. Perhaps we
can awaken the analysts to ascribe any
abortive assaults to the ambiance, or to
perhaps encourage bucolic back street
big spenders to show some
identification, the area being not too
healthy for tourists, missionaries or
anyone not showing the proper scars.
This is not a theme park and you may
be ill prepared for the predations and
likely predicaments you will
encounter.

This is just some friendly advice,
describing in the most vague terms the
tools and hazards of the trade. That
anonymous gimmick doesn't work
when the locals don't give a shit and
you get a tap on the shoulder
reminding you that indeed we are just
spirit made flesh and bound to suffer
the usual indignities, the implication
being that the polite form is hoping

that there's no imposition but just the same here's the ticket to elimination. This ferocious atmosphere is losing sunlight every second.

The labyrinth is just one opinion it draws you left and right and tempts you with the usual cheese it brings you forth by way of its inevitability and not by any path other than the turn of a stone or the inclination of an eye. At the end who knows—paradise island mystery dancers? The imagination a mere silhouette. The final mystery of the mountains. The face behind the wheel that leaves with a smile. The indigo light that blurs the horizon and continues the illusion of what is and what could be.

So how straight is a straight line? Attitude and altitude are the keys, a matter of perspective, when a seemingly innocuous event in your eyes is the trauma of another existence, that creates the lifelong aversion or conversion, and perhaps even a

sideways glance creates a twitch,
sunny corners avoided, the need for a
periscope, an umbrella a bullet proof
car the high wall encrusted with glass
an unlisted number no forwarding
address the need for protection more
than usual even in this day and age.
Twisted voices echo up from the
angled metal, burning up time in
transit, under linoleum floors where
cockroach colonies nest among day of
infamy headlines. You watch the
rumble and think you can dance.

9

Diabolical plots hatched by upset
connections, the outpost seminaries
yielding premonitions of a toothy grin
appearance, the greeting indigenous,
nefarious and leading one to the
obvious conclusion that it might be
time to liquidate a few incurably
frozen assets and hit the road.
Heretical symbolists confuse the order
of their triads, placing the inherent
lamp atop the convivial tripod, a tip of
the hat to the revisionists, never too
late for an excuse. They were out to
suppress the need to travel through
midnight daydreams, to complete the
cycle begun by the temptations of the
latent image, the visual surgeon
tripping as he's skipping past the light
table, operating too skillfully with dull
knife, rainbow colored pills spilling
out his coat, taking in the dictation of
the nurse whose hair got into the
incision, a kind face above the plastic
net, smiling with the usual lipstick on
the teeth. The nurse she stroked my
neck with an alcohol soaked swab and

gave me the needle whispering
biological nonsense into my ear,
chalky orderlies hang in muttering
groups outside the rain filled roof
selling drugs to passersby, the
administrator up the stairs kicking
around the abacus, the volunteers
smiling in many intricate positions,
their deposits already buying war
bonds for the next crusade, the
ambulances rolling the victims piling
in.

Citizens in cages never deter the lame
dogs from making haste away from
clouds of tear gas, their crocodile
lamentations rolling down cheeks like
marbles on a tilted floor, the
redemption centers all closed down
their tin roof dripping after the tornado
departs, the attic filled with green
stamps, glue pots stuck to palettes of
artists who lack only a tongue, their
long brush strokes filled with burrs and
late night railroad thistles, pleading for
one last canvas one more gouache
before the diner closes its doors, where

the white line straddler fended off
hostile locals awaiting the dawn, the
prospect safe in some paneled room
wondering when the door at the
bottom of the stairs might close.

Eager refusals are hard to deny, even
harder to match with equal malcontent,
when the contention is to break the
nation of empty hands with palms
lined and creased, snapping curves
inscribed by incisive legalists hoping
for one last stab into Caesar's long
dead corpse, on the gulf, where low
drawls comment on the water skiing
conditions and calculate the cost of the
short term call, where drunken sailors
tug on empty jugs, where ankles are
bandaged against the rain, where
distant thunder projects the image of a
flash flood undermining the trailer
again, where turtles and rabbits flee in
consternation, where the time to haul
the last shambles is always half past
nine.

Such wondrous deeds, such great
escapes, incredible leaps of faith, a
new indoor one hundred yard dash
record, the final pipeline, the longest
drought without substantial rain, the
world's most difficult tongue twister, a
delightful new use for peaches, a
prolonged scream, double the
fascination for immersion, experiential
environments, the final tedium, the
unraveling of the crowd, the cross
town bus, the first drops of melting
snow. Wild strawberries grow naked
under the midnight sun, the authorities
have made a deal with the weatherman
to predict nothing but detention and
dysentery, the stalls lacking doors thus
decorum. It was a moral, no, an
ethical, no, a transcendental success,
an aesthetic accomplishment, perhaps
barricade breaking, perhaps we should
just overthrow the whole mess who
knows what may come. The sewers
clogged with crumbled letters of
discontent, the promises of little faith
healers peddling the ultimate in
redemption toys, broken shards of

pottery in some abandoned
archeological dig.

10

Hardly had hardly the first word been spoken when the transcription began, the threat of repetition ever present, the alphabet restrained the lithographs poured forth and we were treated to analogy and simile and circumlocution, logic oppressing the ravings, but hey it's just a sideline to keep us in grape. Most is cast aside as the technology changes and the whole mess mutates attempting to make it relevant pretty unlikely a bad practical joke it's something to do. The sounds of the jukebox are too intense they require definition pills some order some character development what do you think this is, some true Christian spirit? Driving low riding cars through next week's mutton shotgun farmers laying low under the sullen wind, the hubcaps rattle on long gone shacks the inevitable license plate from 68 the numb fingers drawing shredded fabric around sloping shoulders, come back later when the real frost comes over the plains.

The stallion's long sloping neck drew the gaze to its flaring red surrounded eye, fixed on that light bulb that sears through the wax paper shade, a compliance with standards drawn up through dog reconciliation, leaning peacefully on the cactus, spines electric in the gray afternoon, swaying with the wind, that numb somnambulist, seeking his airline stewardess, peaceful now on the sloping gravel along the high mountain pass, the road leading the weary traveler to dead ends on the edge of the world and hey, ain't this nothin' but the middle of nowhere?

11 _____

This is the place where gravel from the
receding truck kicks up to threaten
your glasses, where distant thunder
from dark clouds are the only light on
the road, where the clouds bluff but
rain never falls, where the streaks so
far have missed wide of their mark.
That hidden valley ghost town begins
with a ten minute video that tells the
tale of madness gone south, where you
never quite understand what the
proprietress wants, where the curios
line the walls and dust tells you that
not a buyer had been found since the
access road was shunted off the
interstate, where forlorn civilizations
grasp for the last pennies of the tourist
trade.

Pot belly stoves burn on the edge of
the burning woods, gullies and
trickling streams bring the hunter's
crushed beer cans down with the
spring thaw, where songbirds arrive
too late for the feast and the postcard
from Custer's Last Stand gets faded in

the bristling sun. That green bar
glowed above the pool hall, the faces
all bathed in blue, the creaking door
and hushed laughter in anticipation of
the inevitable flare-up, the frozen
stillness the flashlight that scissors the
gloom, the shouting from the stairs the
voices real but the forms hidden,
surveillance being the only way to
assume control. Obsessions were
neatly arrayed in cupboards, displays
only the fetish sadist could afford,
being implements of nineteenth
century medicine, the owner precise in
his overpricing with little patience for
the uninitiated. But those who could
see that light came in droves,
fascinated by the objects of their
desire, all in the knowledge that the
sunrise would bring no relief from the
semaphore catastrophe.

To think, there were once woods here,
now just crumpled cars in the ditch and
bodies arrayed and shivering in the
purple dawn. The artifacts and the
outcasts played out their tiny dramas,

being a full-length melodrama on the
melting screen, the crowd clapping
mechanically and interrupting the
unfolding mess. The insults were
delineated and the agents aligned, the
various furies associated with the state
came buzzing around their ears. The
border patrol took all afternoon
fondling a bottle of aspirin and some
vitamin C caps, looking disappointed
when they handed back our disheveled
packs, fearful eyes winking through
fallen flesh, as the sun went down and
all hopes of further transport collapsed.
We were stuck on the border with no
hope of surprise, so retreated to a
laundromat to further polish our
exterior, hoping they wouldn't
recognize us the following day of
course having jettisoned the offending
articles.

Twelve midnight, lights out and a
madman at the wheel. Straddling the
white line blinking burn-out eyes,
those sudden blots revealing a harsh
landscape, open oven city, radio

signals crossing that blaring preacher damming all souls not on his path with top 500 oldies station out of Tijuana with bottom of the ninth nobody on, with plaintive wail of brake fluid gone dry and big Texas radio hoe-down, today's sermon: after the attack, when we emerged with brandished souls from the post industrial rubbish heap, sending postcards to no one bragging, "the climate it is lovely and the women they wear no tops."

Temporal enthusiasts conspire with some ephemeral cause, our now antiquated somnambulist is turning tricks to help increase the dosage of bootleg sensitivity sessions, the equilibrium long upset by navigating tremor competitions, when the first being the last and the last nowhere in sight made no difference because nobody had a scorecard making it difficult to keep track of today's most outrageous event. Canned laughter from the salmon factory the fish have all gone upstream, a tape loop drones:

"all systems go", making the heartless telegraphers change everything but the last line. The terse statement was a concise note that drove our heroes to make that last, fateful swan dive.

12_____

Never look to the military for anything
too profound sure the weaponry is
quite sophisticated but basically it's all
brute force and they keep jabbering
about the ultimate sacrifice until
there's not one lamb left to slaughter.
The call came from the big muddy the
fragging party slept through the
ceremony and of course the call for
calm was ignored for what reason
should we stay calm? It's always code
orange here in the big apple and if it
goes red alert watch out for your
gasoline tank, anybody found in lotus
position risks trampling as everyone
starts rushing out the front door.

Some four-star war criminal felt
compelled to comment before the great
unleashing, his mad dogs showing no
civility if it sounds familiar just read
your history and no comments from
those about to hit the front.

"Lord knows we've tried to do our best
to create motherless children shoving

their snotty noses into our blatant
coronations, home sweet home won't
be what it used to be when we get
done, watching you beat the ground
with Sunday's bloody paper, the
shredded edition the arrogant
resentment the population masters
foresworn to our righteous duty. Our
systematic uniqueness pushes
inhalation before you can ever catch
your breath, poetic duels produce
victims among the ultimately killed
bystanders. The outlook for all you big
time losers is that you'll run out of
money before your game goes down.
Honestly, how you paid for things now
that you're finding it a bit different,
never leaving your house without your
comfortable grandfather, the legacy of
silence and defeat, the shuffling of
twice read papers, the eerie calm after
the bomb, the entreaties in gazebos,
the loosened brake causing the car to
run down the street and the comic
parade chasing it and yelling somehow
thinking their calling will stop it on its

inevitable parade. Why, it's the latest word in the chips are down.

"Tell us about your dogs, we've had them for years, an alarming state, but reduction of the considerate service of approval by the council of aggressive expenditures is only to be expected. What's your opinion? I really couldn't give a shit, nothing but options and pure aid and a giveaway on the energy drains, the treasury bare there is no realistic figure for the unworkable bitterness that follows. No children will inherit this dreadful spirit, no ears will hear the moon's tiptoe eclipse, no eyes will witness the breath's last gasping. Dawn to dusk curfews, I can assure you the night life is wild in the smoldering city."

13_____

Rumors spread through the
deconstruction site that face shields
worn thin extend and blend the
overland journey where the chief
attractions are sawed off shotguns and
hawkish eyes scanning for something
to do while waiting for the inevitable
bus, the pursuit of some obsession
shared by none proclaims some
principal denied by all in the know.
Swatting flies in the coffee shop the
cockroach waving his antennae in
stagnant hello, the servants of the
forlorn industrialists are forced to live
upstairs, where the roof always leaks
and the tenants downstairs swear and
bang brooms on ceilings where paint
peels with every step. The only
restaurant in town collapsed a roof
beam in the salad bar the police
advising the weary traveler to refrain
from going downtown last night's riots
having put a dent into the shopping
mall. Waiter there's a telephone cable
in my soup and I can't seem to make
the connection.

Stolen gray mornings sifted gently through the lattice of personalities that call it home, idle spiders eyeing fallen angels with gossamer wings stranded on the uptown crossing without a transfer to tomorrow. Larcenous jackals tread lightly in harlequin tiptoe collapse, rising with the moon and riding through the wheat field's golden light, suspended timeless in the outlaw's sullen breast, the desert heat waving from across the way creating images on the road to the unapproachable mountain that always looms on the horizon but there's never a road that gets you there. The winter wind causes thirst for an early spring, while above the timber line frozen streams in stasis like silken sheets for the season wrapped. Flickering light plays across the valley on messianic afternoons, making the ramblers turn sideways to see straight ahead, it's all a dubious return operation prolonged by mistaken identity, a continual nascent topic no one dares discuss, resurrecting the dread spirit in hidden clauses that even the smallest print cannot reveal. Arms stretch akimbo to blind the mind's eye and settle for nothing in the end, all time given over to rattling around in boxes make a hasty retreat with barely a nod to the possibilities of what stands around the corner, misplacing terminology in the mirror's hollow stare.

The determination of pleasure in the latter stages is by instinctive and casual turns in response to foreign stimuli, a hurtling of massive integrity insults at every side trip, leaving smoldering synapses in comic disarray, all connections coming a few seconds too late so the subject's gone when the shutter finally snaps. Calloused fingers grasp fantasy replicas of living and breathing and possibly sentient beings, all parts strewn on the living room floor, a moment of doubt about what costume fits today's crime. Seemingly all is a better proposition than meddling with some adopted ethos,

and they have the nerve to call this
evolution. Emergency only phone
numbers posted on the lavatory wall,
swollen ears listening intently to the
latest whine, a demand on time that
crushes life. The crowd buzzes on the
collapsing pier, mumbles about some
zodiacal confluence, some showdown
that faded in the misty dawn, some gas
station neon on the last road to a
wavering mind. Fingers that grasp
stretch a thousand miles away from the
agony of the unknown and tempt the
seductive horizon to create a blistering
red silhouette, unsuitable chairs
arrayed around the mocking reception,
confused street cars and the wall that
later stood under the flood, the tale
always complicated by the insertion of
the variable character.

At frozen altitudes plotters weave their
vests, ignoring the northern lights,
while serious hawks inscribe parabolas
on the indifferent sky, they see past
peaks to the alluvial plane, there to
spread among mossy crags creased

with sudden rain, shuttered shacks
rattling hub caps, jackrabbits leaning
on fence posts and a winking cactus on
the edge of the Continental Divide,
where snow falling all winter could
meditate whether to head east or west
once the big thaw begins.

14_____

Armageddon's horseless riders made a left turn three lights after the apocalypse, gray limbs hung in napalm's harness, snatching looks in the wilderness and realizing that only a treeless land would rise once again. All phrases are designed to muddle the linkage between what was going on and who was running the show. Perhaps it's all a vague attempt to satirize fascism and to reveal its made over corporate face. But this veiled and low-key romp through the verbal factory has as much effect as picketing a library because it holds too many books. Those are minds on hold in there punctuated by their crumbling covers, walk in and you can hear them whispering their loneliness to the walls. Give them that lackadaisical toothy grin and rub the eyes with black, the local artist rendering those typical landscapes can obscure anything that gets in the way of the tourist board's pitch. Those photos as

well where everyone stands in a row
who was taking that picture anyway?

15_____

Creaking door through the barking dog
stairwell darkness, graffiti on the
catacomb walls, porous rock dripping
limestone sentiments to coyote face
masks, clocks running backwards these
private observations tell of a different
time. The advocate of eating thoughts
will take possession of any
masterpiece left dangling, a
manipulation process that intrigues to
deliver romantic lyrics, emerging from
the cacophony in the chamber made
for deliverance of any intrepid soul as
it stumbles along this nebulous path.

So beat that retreat and fade to black,
turn that corner that page that card
over and in a blink of an eye delve into
other realms all a hasty and cheap
allusion to mortality a fib concealed in
unkempt markets a strap that holds a
tenuous breeze a conclusion reached
when brushing your teeth the fleas
flying in the circus with no big top.
Yield or stand fast affirm or deny beat
on hollow logs to send dramas through

the airy palms on the stage where the
curtain never parts. Patient demands
remain unheeded, whispers contrive to
draw conclusions, fingers tap out tunes
on mellow keys, the chorus brought
the house down when they all read
from different scores. The light's
failing haven't paid the bill, a
collection of miscreants await the
garbled wisdom spewed out in nightly
sessions designed to draw out the
misery, it's making a fast buck to say
the least a poor choice of hat, an
unfortunate turn of the toe only to end
up in the bog with the frog and no
transfer out until midnight.

Anonymous moans clutter the corridor,
the slow step with the carved cane, a
wink coming from nowhere perhaps in
recognition perhaps not or maybe just
a twitch and a smirk. The bells rang all
night the operator out of luck, the
winter fire out by now laden with ice
the handshake perfunctory at best.
These woods will never be cleared but
the shades of gray cast in the hollows

greet the driver no longer responding
the car in a ditch the head met the
glass.

Pictures made by the sun sprawl in the
grass wait and see what develops. The
fumes and the nitrate turn your fingers
black, the wave broken in many colors,
the backpack of delights scattered on
the sands. Those drawings were
meticulous but pointless, the primaries
unmixed the logic obscure and the
museum opens at dawn. No reflections
just the glint of steel angling back and
interfering with taxis huddled by the
riverside, overcharging the
unsuspecting tourist on the scenic
route around the harbor.

Across the water the city sparkled and
filled with hope the journey begins, the
night filled with noise echoing from
the day, the folk emerged despite the
obstacles, their collective drift now a
headlong fleeing, no sense of direction
amidst the hostile impairments. A soft
glance on the soggy parade ground, the

big delay while they fill the trains, the carnival booths glitter, the tires thump on the cobblestones, the first coffee at the morning café. A distant whip cracks the dawn while old men reciting verse litter the concrete with their visitations.

16_____

Be still. Me thinks me hears a rustling, a coalition of forms, a slight brushing of the scrub, a nefarious tiptoe down under the ledge, a fast scramble when the light gets too bright. Those other wobblers, those bereft of conscience, those others we read about so often have gotten less shy and sniff the air in the hopes of a cast-off bag into which they can snuggle their schnozz hoping for at the least a whiff of *etwas zu fressen*. No, my shipwreck, fear not their approach for they are figments and fragments of a past long gone, come to haunt us in our ministrations and file oblique references to their presence hoping for a few lines in the dreary manuscript. They come to spill their gray lifetimes into our jaundiced ears, to invoke the muse of disrespect, to stagger in their side stepping way and convince you and I they are more than just the beached bandits they truly are. They come to convince us that they would give their sole begotten life to some all night consumption gang, to

swan dive with their misrepresented
linguistics off yon precipice yodeling
about the pink sands long lost and their
hopeful, gleaming sunrises. These
cracks in the surface are filled with
peering eyes, waiting so patiently for
you to shuffle off this mortal coil,
thinking I might leave some tender
morsel unmasticated. Saddest
collection of bags of bones you've
ever seen, they handcuff their
miserable possessions to their
bandaged wrists, all on the slow spiral
waiting for the tide's lottery to whisk
them off to endless checker games in
fascist convenience. Their guard dogs
uncollared, they bang on bars and puke
in the cold dawn, they pearl dive in our
illustrious sea, their prize morsel an
irritation to the oyster, they sit like
anchors down there after some
practical jokers pour cement in their
shoes and wish them bon voyage as
they slip them overboard.

But for the sake of the narrative we'll
let all those faces push down into

mine, all coming from somewhere, all swept along with the fortunes of the surf, all ranting and raving from some back alley, wrecked and reeking, wandering through ancient graveyards behind the green subway tunnel, fighting off junkie alligators with swizzle sticks and Sunday's shredded edition, playing dead on the kitchen floor their head in the oven the gas being long ago turned off for non-payment of the utility bill. What drama.

But we must not castigate these forlorn souls as they have come on long journeys down streets in somebody else's winter town. They don raincoats and sneakers in the worst blizzard sing '98, yearning with eyes sunken at billboards of smiling women pointing to the object of their desire, doubting the predictions made for them by ignoble bishops their veins pulsing under blue street lamps their last train gone their dogs chasing any bitch in heat.

Have you ever considered the latest
fashions as you adjust that newspaper
you use for lining your shoes and
jacket on these frosty nights? Have
you seen bundles of wool stare out at
you from doorways offering cold wind
and loneliness if you cared to get
involved? Have you knocked on doors
your frostbitten knuckles making each
rap softer? Have you seen the faces in
bleak lobbies beseeching money,
cigarettes, time, where the dusty plants
droop during reruns of last year's
fights? Have you seen the lonely
hunter conned by lack of instincts and
a telescopic lens? Have you sipped the
lukewarm petroleum by-product that
passes for ambrosia these days, the cup
shredded the liquid running out like a
short loan on tomorrow?

17_____

But despite our unspoken protestations here they come. They come out, they come out, out of all the one horse farms and two lane highways, from the bus depots and all night diners, from freight yards and strip-mined hills, out to our sandy beach, our endless plains, out from their mother's bloody womb they come. To rest at the red light and adjust their rear view mirrors, unsure and unhappy about what's behind. To stand and be counted when no one is counting at all, to fight for what was right when they were all wrong, to draw their columns on the bathroom wall, to hear the great orator only to discover he was a humming machine, the carrier wave overcoming every syllable and the words incomprehensible, to find life where it had been abandoned and left askew in some echo played out long ago on stage and screen.

Their street throws neon light in the rain. The peddlers come with their wares throwing them down long flights of stairs. They are akimbo at the bottom laughing like it was all a big joke, the straight and narrow divulging that there's nothing but nocturnal resurgence in the big death wish, the rooftop acrobatics all to no avail. Listen my *compadres*, the mission has closed its doors, freedom fighters have stolen all the manhole covers and the old line about twenty dollars or twenty days has always been answered by: haven't got a dime and can't spare the time.

What, no grunt acknowledgement that jellyfish savagery surfaces even in dying seas, that moon faces glow hardship restlessness, that geisha girls got Coca Cola transfusions, that you have sat shamefaced in the all night back booth temple and desecrated the bishop's penny-eyed calculations? Even you lot must admit that the square is bursting at the seams and if it doesn't morph circle wise soon that it will be out of touch with the universe.

This pale proximity to promiscuous laxity defies the morbid layer of felicity that's somehow been maintained, we sensitive nerve clusters keep our nasal passages clean with as many street corner hydraulics as we can muster. Your behavior in our fair state is grounds for divorce in any honky paradise, as flys battle for the disgrace of eating our shipwreck's face, his main line stamping out platitudes in our gear flux ratios.

Shall we kindle a smoky fire—this shit's always so wet—and relate to our lemmings that now's the time to be free, to refuse the insinuations on their divine credentials, to cast off makeshift labels, to refuse to be the fodder for theories of mass extermination? That's a dangerous hypothesis but hold it up to a mirror and you'll see it smiling back at you, or perhaps you'll just see some letters and your usual scowl. That old chest in the attic is filled with rusty emblems, the old fur coat where flea and lice

playfully glide, the swirling beast that
snacks on midnight ghosts, the
cringing moon providing its usual dim
and deceptive light. There at the
bottom sit the photographs of the
ditches of the last great war, the lost
children of Babylon's whore, the
spurning at every door, the inevitable
face on the barroom floor. But Saint
Joan's still tied to the stake because the
believers ran out of matches, the
submarine's gone down with open
hatches, the crew having the disease
nobody catches and all seeing light,
and life, but only in snatches. Born
onto death; borne away with a breath.

Our gathering brethren are all the
geeks, gooks, highway ramblers, souls
unrestful, misbegotten children,
hunchback somnambulists, anarchy
peddlers, confused artifacts coming in
from the outposts of windowless back
alleys, toll road dawns, dumpster
banquets. They sense grievous
misjudgment somewhere along the
line, all being lateral variations cast off

from the harlot mismatch factory,
holding on to contradictions and the
mixed message, like beauty soap for
Nagasaki's spoiled child.

Trace along the page now with your
long, delicate fingers, the nails painted
a soft glowing blue, and find the
embryo of your future self inverting
and twisting through the changing
chords of some forgotten melody,
those single notes echoing in the
swamp, the steady drizzle the basso
continuo the sound of stalking
footsteps down a sloping ridge to
ponds where antiphonal birds watch
concentric circles by the raindrops
formed, last year's faded leaves a
mattress for your weary head, the color
a mad impressionist weeping before
his empty canvas the uselessness of
emulating creation, the wordless water
splashing down grass lined gullies the
soft mist through the pine trees.

18_____

The whirling dervish on his last spin settles his eyes on a neon sign that sparks an overland journey, his sodden robes awaiting the passing of rain under the overpass, a hostile crew beckons him forth for a long ride to meet some sullen uncle who has pawned their radio even before they arrive. On the way he met Bible peddlers trying to convince him that he did something bad before dinner, the hawker not having a good day all around as he was trailed throughout the afternoon by a giggling street girl who kept flicking ashes from her roach into his collection box. His pensive parishioners were all waiting to wade across the Styx, his ever-faithful altar boys languishing in silken robes watching it all go down on the six o'clock report. (The stink about the soccer riots ran headlong into the refugees from the front the detergent showed up and made all clean.)

Our lad raised on Rumi hesitates,
while flickering gray light snaps at the
wind-swept messianic afternoon, him
standing sideways on the tilting floor,
his mental tasks carjacked by a case of
mistaken identity, even the mongoose
has doubts when first glimpsing the
cobra's threatening cowl.

Lipstick stained cigarette butts carpet
the floor, a true gutter snipe's worst
nightmare, heaving chests sighing
behind the barroom door, the nascent
topic being the shrug before dawn, the
mind's eye blinded by the sure thing,
all reflected confusion in the fatal
mirror's hollow stare. He thought this
a better proposition than cold cereal in
steel cages, but the number he'd been
given to call in case of dire emergency
had been disconnected, all the
operators gone, all the connections
lost, all the cooks having hit the road
with their woks to join the Red Guard.
He stretched his fingers ten thousand
miles and gave it a whirl, his spin

seeking solace on his bodily border
where seductive horizons marked the
void, where red wine afternoons
caused him to wake in some dim park,
his left sandal inexplicably gone.

He met sullen schoolboys in faded
black raincoats who spent their
familial afternoons plotting activities
that upset the syllabus, pursed lips
murmuring scripts horrible,
misbegotten plans making the
sensational compromise, tense legs
shifting, handing out bloody
manifestos inside the wicked
warehouse, nodding out under pool
tables awaiting the last game of nine
ball, that long flight of stairs waving
goodbye in the library, where tonight's
last wise guy never saw the dawn.

He twirled on and fell out in
overstuffed chairs in a hotel lobby
where there never are any free rooms,
the clerk yawning while ambulances
come and go tearing the lace curtain

during the transfers, the words stopped
all the crowd could do was stare.

Meanwhile, cross town in the
elimination zone clean cut leather lads
threaten a drag queen with bodily
harm, she edges them on by flicking
cigarette ash into their carburetors,
while armed and dangerous
government agents frisk frail old
women buying postage stamps, the
unclaimed luggage causing them to
clear the terminal. They found alien
fingerprints on the crucifix, the power
cables all cut ceasing the hum but
arcing blue in the back pasture.

His time passed slowly in the umbrage
zone, so he adjusted his shades and
didn't give it all a second glance. If
you're born here and leave it you'll
never miss it if you can't stop in just
smile as you go by. The bar is busy
only when the hunters hit town, but
they soon depart leaving pieces of
squirrel plastered all over the trees. He
learned to keep moving otherwise the

lumber company might have mistaken
him for a tree.

Some latent symbol sounded and the
tomb carvers pause with their chisels
on high, the pedestrians played
bullfighter with passing cars, we
pissed our initials on the Senate steps.
Fortune's high card was on the table
but he failed to recognize the game,
the fix being in he flopped about like a
fish in a boat sinking into the loam up
to his knees. Stuck he was but his eyes
landed on a milky spider web blowing
in the soft breeze the sun making
pearls of the woven prey. The final,
sweet smell of the air. The smooth
stones of the stream just above the
surface made hot by the sun. The
inevitable waterfall.

Four thousand grad students blazed
away at inverse variations, the
backroom boys working out the
logistics of the desert maneuvers,
naturally playing it all up as a holy
war. Wine bottles sat like judges on

the shelf's tribunal, the swift
mechanics doubting the sensibility of it
all, their maligned efficiency a result
of an unworthy consortium, the
legalistic view smiling through glass
panes adorned with visions of
mediocrity, nodding yes, we are
closed, come back with another
identity, leave your flimsy credentials
in the out box and hit the road. A limp
form caressed the feeble switch,
hawkers selling ladyfingers to halfwit
cannibals, the rowdy assembly bowing
before the ruler's bluff, his implacable
mumbo jumbo trying to keep
everything under control. He has
refurbished the ugly deities but the
robes are slipping revealing the same
tired three-chord rock and roll.

Any perceptive palette would have
puked at the first take, that frameless
picture run amok in the masochistic
museum. Congenital symbiosis,
thermostatic stasis, the genius of Eros
bypassed the collective jive, it being
the heart and soul of the dogma posed

by the internal upset gang. Low and mean prowl car under the elevated tracks, blue sparks fall into the snow, there is little patience held by the horde, the oil rights are rigged, the heretics making their last furious stand.

His final attempt at spinning only increased the torque screwing himself deeper into the earth, observed by glazed eyes staring out of windows filled with dying plants. Cause and effect are drowned, the didactic among them concluding that a spinner might have many turning points in his life, that the final twist under that leafy tree can only be a contortion of logic and sequence that is tossed to the winds and explodes behind as we speed through the streets tossing our Molotov cocktails out the car window.

Creaking door through the barking dog stairwell darkness, graffiti on the catacomb walls, porous rocks drip limestone sentiments onto coyote face masks, ten clocks running backwards all telling a different time. The Master of the Ecce Homo Masterpiece draped his form along the winding stairs, the viewers a blur, the sanguine students, the mild interludes of romantic lyricism, the emergence from the cacophony, the chamber made to deliver the wandering soul from its nebulous quest.

Silver moments. Watch movements. Underwater quiet drifting in slow motion down the escarpment. Tortoise shell colors. Pollen exploding from windswept trees to ride on the west wind to midnight meetings in the sullen swamp, whispering to our graceful turner that this, thank god, be thy home.

19_____

What's this my shipwreck, a flurry
from you, a stirring all right maybe
just a twitch, but I see you are intent
on learning of our ways, of
deciphering the codes long ago
obscured, of even some hesitant hope
and glimmering of understanding.
There is no alternative you share what
you don't want to share you lose track
of time you feed the traditional baby
the same token in every country, all of
this is a mere backdrop proving that
everyone is good at one thing. Call it
natural causes call it lethargic
commands call it a blazing neon sign
through the catacomb of hard knocks,
call it immunization against the disease
nobody catches, call for a doctor and
see how far that gets you.

In the orchestra of life we share the
stage with consumptive reed players
always grasping for that last note, that
double high C just their luck as the
conductor who wasn't there punched
his last ticket and nodded down to the

dusty bar rail and slipped in the mud, waving his baton furiously the band way out of tune, wandering in the concert hall banished from the cheap seats, deaf musicians scaling the unthinkable ladder, crossing the longitude on a tide of shifting sands.

My herbal knowledge is renowned thus I will brew you a concoction known by its certain smell often used by flotillas of semi-conscious ravens who cruise the aqueduct looking for misread sentiments, the culmination of all that effort is a loose knit connivance that herds all the mister nice guys into the stockade of blatant substance. It's a bit of the ephemeral mind rot on moist Thursdays only, visiting hours being suspended while they clear the ward of the last bad idea that swept through town.

But hold, I have received a garbled dispatch from the slaughterhouse front. It seems we've attained complete

victory and can step on anybody's
calloused neck and call the shots when
they invoke their deities or we were
routed our religion changed like
somebody pulled the rug from under
the Grecian urn and the pottery's
spilled all over the linoleum and we
have to wave goodbye to:

Sylvan glades of tasseled dancers,
wedding parties with fog bound
ghosts, sample case nostalgia and the
hierarchy of light, playful surgeons
and their Ethiopian knives, ornate
saturation, the fat free diet, compulsive
urges to cure foreigners of their
dissolving preferences, the meandering
syncopation of basement dance tunes,
the combustion that freezes the hearty
combatant, fatal songs glorifying
tenuousness, thumbnails ripping the
vital video, clutching the silver cliff
and reaching for the final strawberry
while the tiger awaits smiling above
(with a tip of the hat to Zenophobia),
morbid fisherman who send icy
glances to the first mate, crippled

mileage experts, heavenly grace at the
drop of a hat, green bottle reflections
and the melting mind, substitutions for
the real thing, tales of fascist
amelioration, clumsy popes spilling the
beans, the football coach tearful in the
train depot, blown chances and beer
cans under the porch, hybrid
individualists grabbing identity where
they can, ermine collars and the shrug
in the strobe's glare, cracked lips
seeking new blood, tape recorders
cooling their tubes, two-bit home
grown, spitting leaflets (a nice base for
kindling), horses with blinders on
tightropes to tomorrow.

So we have our choice of poisons:
This one shrinks your corpuscles we
call it the axe murderer special, this
one cause a mild rash causes you to
lose your big toe so you fall into
traffic, this one sheds your hair and is
said to cause nervousness in sunlight,
our upper-downer is a yo-yo on the
mood swings, pretty nasty as it makes
you want to slit your wrists and then

ten seconds later a twisted smile comes
to wry lips, this one ingratiates you to
parasites, like a whole bunch of
relatives show up one summer's eve
and demand to know what's for dinner,
the last being one of our favorites it's
so musical causing instant repetition of
every syllable you ever spoke in a
language you don't understand, we set
one such rap to a world beat and the
impression was quite stark, the tenor
shoving his fingers down his throat to
stop the inevitable flow of genetic
repercussions, no more Danny Boy at
the end of the rainbow.

So drink the brew and wave goodbye
to all the tedious horseshit filed in the
stool pigeon's cabinet, that leech
ignorance putrifying in the Platonic
cave.

20_____

So my friend we have come to the point where it's time to repeat our admonition about the fostering of any malcontent. Don't think I'm kidding when I say that time does not exist, it's just a numbers game invented by some Nordic prankster in need of a new gimmick, a trick that once sold down the river will never return with the tide. If you leave this place you had better know that there is a better place. Can't you imagine how it feels seeing you suffer? Do you think it's easy? What difference does it make whose angst is being driven by what force, or are we going to spend the rest of our time together arguing about it? Taking into consideration that I'll never give you an excuse, and you certainly can't give one to me, do we have to prove that this test tube is anything but the universe checking out the possibilities and finally giving up with a shrug that maybe the next time out we'll do better? How can you sit there in a heap knowing that somebody is going to be killed in the next two minutes? I'm just trying to save you the trouble of working it through. When you get to whatever you deem as heaven are you really going to yearn to come back to this swamp and tell everybody how great the final payout is? And when you're high and happy do you really care how miserable everybody else might be? I can bet you're not going to take the chance. The last guy who tried that ended up nailed to a cross and his followers eventually hoarded the gold pulled from slave-worked mines and raised money for the vestments using satellites and fear.

21_____

But I digress. I have a senseless
appointment whose urgency floats
through a haze of recognition, a
bottom fog that takes all morning to
burn off from the hollows, a note sent
with twisted images, a mindset flying
over the park with knowing glances
and naked love in some bubbling
stream. All twisted history, all making
sense of the wreck in the ditch. If you
could move you might come with me
to the volcano to hear the world
digesting, to see the heretical monk
who proclaims that to affirm the truth
once in a lifetime leads to salvation
(the children following him as he
bangs his drum), to observe those
bright colors and shining eyes, those
harlequin heels those jangle boots that
go click clack with castanet steps on
waxen floors in the crystal hallway, the
juggler of grapes describing appetizing
and intricate patterns on the curved
stairway, the royal kennel baying at the
moon, those Tarot mosaic ceilings. We
always think that in the past we were

all aristocrats, while in truth we sat
with bad lungs on muddy floors staring
into empty bowls, sighing ahh, the
good old days.

Contrapuntal heartbeats the rhythm of
the young lover's bed, we watched the
barges on the river from the rooftop,
the soft clang of bells sounding every
time she shook her bandaged wrist. We
floated down slate bottomed streams to
an appointment with shimmering
afternoons, dusty sunbeams dotting the
forest floor as we sighed with soft
chords and fell into orbit around the
moon. The church of the woods is
better unbuilt, a cathedral in any misty
hollow already stands, mushroom
sacraments there for free, the sunrise
gospel enough.

Rights performed in covens, the last
outposts of the silent human league,
dark forces conspire to raise the dread
forces, stayed by compassionate hands
placed on the glowing orb.

22_____

But first some descriptive aside, some setting of the tone some oblique reference to whispers in the corridors of the powerless. We must endeavor to conquer the snide obelisk, the cornucopia of festive improvisation, when we sit with the motor running a heap of mold on the back seat and we ask the copper for a drink to wash it down. These are nothing but historical references quoted endlessly just some forcibly entered statistical analysis. This is my third time around and last time some sagging clown got the bright idea that sensational duality empties the conceptual deed snatcher, that if you ring the bloody towel in dinosaur innocence some vestigial chromosomes will hang out pitching pennies on street corners it's just something to do. Our next victim dragged on the exploding cigar and crossed his eyes on the waiting room divan, all the while mumbling incantations to his ugly deities, sealing indecipherable messages into green bottles and tossing them off our surly strand.

Considering that the possibilities are endless, that you can become nervous in dawn's cold light when soft footsteps make their way through doorways where shadows are strewn, where shredded wine bottle eyes stare at the cobblestone mosaic, where cars melt into the river side drive, where all manholes turn to mandallas, where carnivorous eye shifters chase ornate thoughts through windowless alleys all waiting for the daily news, where questioning children tap shoulders and turn everyone into a two year old, where the moon with its halo races behind the clouds, where smoldering cities sit empty, evacuated behind the billboards of eternal distaste. The aristocrats squat on the ballroom floor, their corsages wilted in the smoky atmosphere, bright red flashing in the fog rolling contest.

Here's some constant input. There was
a lapse in the phase of fossil hearsay
and larcenous demons fostered
individual mismanagement, the key to
it all being the forgotten laugh, a brief
moment when the desert sunflower
vibrates in the Mojave, when a quiet
hand weaves soul mate glances down
the endless plane, a casual touch in a
crowded bus, the sun blazing a white
dot into the back of the eye, a quiet
sailboat a skeleton crew the current
handling the rudder and the wind the
speed.

It's probable that combinations of
disaster court the likelihood of despair,
yet all in all it's something we all can
share, bitching about the empty
swimming pool, it simply isn't fair.

Resonant time quotations in the
midnight market, unkempt profiles in
the overflowing filing cabinet, it's all
inside. Tap the underground river find
the sweet cool water drink in its calm

darkness and let your toes drift there
on these hot days.

23_____

So there is the wall and here are the faces. Windows like eyes of the dragon with too many heads to keep up with, the souls like swords cutting away the joyous, waiting in brick boxes for decisions about the next diversionary tactic. Pick one anyone.

Mister Wide Eyes stares you down all night long at the all night automat, his twenty five cent heart long burned out by rancid coffee, leaning on the linoleum covered table keeping talk to a minimum, he wanders down to the terminal and waits for a train that never leaves, dragging his allegorical overcoat behind him on the marble floor, watching times of arrival and departure change like the odds on life, never blinking always thinking fixing you with his stare by the information booth and you awkward with the goods in your hand, to wander into the tunnels where the buses warm up and fill the tubes with ash.

This gray dog of bereft appearance
saunters uneasily through the terminal
times, he fumbles conspicuously in
shadow doorways for the key to it all,
snapping splintered fingernails like a
locust waiting for the wind, forgetting
what he had come for, so rushed out
and knocked over the begging nun, her
petty change spilling through the bleak
corridors her shaky pitch saving some
punks in some foreign land.

Those electrical fires are a bit out of
control so he sacked the archeological
museum to regain some sense of
immediacy, his fingers like tendrils
seeking the frozen sun, his veins and
capillaries swarming like moths
around the gas station sulphur lamps
on that last run from Amarillo to
Abilene. Some do-gooder tried to haul
him off to the recycling center but was
turned back at the gate.

A vision came to him, the glory of the
past in some bishop's looted crown,
but history's force washed over him

and the full moon tide swept him back
into his loss, which came and went so
suddenly that it left him desolate and
weeping in the cathedral garden. How
can he eliminate those days in the
barbed wire playground, where ragged
sweepers worked in the pouring rain,
his time trials neglected the runner did
a two minute mile but nobody
bothered to consult their watch.

24_____

Or Messenger Phil who ran through
the back door with a snapshot of some
out of focus dog next to a tilting
Christmas tree and those albums filled
with broken down Fords on the
northern rim, pointing proudly to those
too big enlargements of the Arkansas
River where he saw the wanted poster
of Eldridge Cleaver and said, "We
must have crossed that river fourteen
times, the conductor woke me up in El
Paso, that time in Terra Haute, the
Altoona slag heaps, you could reach
out your arm and grab the valley wall,
or was it the Rogue River? It must
have been the North Platte, those
falling rocks, the engravings colored
by a stilled hand, the trains full of
troops my buddies edging me on to my
birthday, the cracked lips of stream
bottoms in the drought, hung up in
Moose Jaw, the Ogden root beer
stands, the trains filled with troops."

After the accident he stooped and
staggered, struggling to remove the

bandages to see what kind of job the technicians had done on his face, the nurse pulling him back into bed shouting into his ear, "You got three phone calls but they were all wrong numbers!" Cold laughter rang from his strangled throat when he finally got a look into the mirror. "Though the back room boys aren't admitting it a piece of the action has been molested from everybody's earth and there's no turning back. There have been feeble bribes accepted and old clients haunted for spare change, their executives turning blue on the lavatory floor reaching for numbers scratched on the stall wall."

Phil wasn't phased by earthquakes but would become unbalanced in the rain, his unsolvable gimmickry put on the shelf and his misdemeanor notions given backdoor idolatry. He became the classic stumblebum *turista* shouting at the eroded mailbox, wiping his forehead in disbelief as to how far things had gone down, cursing

moments of clarity as revelations of
inevitable doom, shuddering with the
cold wind he called his friend, the only
thing the wind ever did for him was
bad lungs and a disposition to match.

He'd seen it all, like masks falling in
the midnight surprise, overturned carts
in street violence smashups, the menial
feasts of hedonistic losers, the
mumbling visage disguised by
harlequin lamps, pretenses of ecstasy
stored in aquariums sold and bought
by any means necessary on the
staccato market. Those faces smiled
and frowned with each turn of the
neck, those hopeless emigrants
stranded on bodily borders, the sulphur
lamps and their orange glare the
sputtering electrical wires jumping in
the air stabbing aimlessly for a ground,
tender bodies crossing the erector set
bridge in a purple fog, lights pulsing,
his vibrating hand stretching out for
seeking fingers to touch, his thousand
mile pilgrimage ending up with some

tourist taking his picture through a rolled up window of some passing car.

Arms fallen to his sides, eyes staring at the sky, weeping in the rain, the ancient farmer turned his head sideways to better hear the locusts' approach.

Phil's nervous nuptials were negotiated with twisted sheets on the back porch floor, always the romantic he raised his eyebrows when he heard the riot torn city shouting his name, his chief burned in effigy, his lethargic legion making a deal with the bouncer who lacked only a neck. But not a twinge of remorse from our drifter, he'd seen the hard times, his blue and calloused knuckles testament enough to the things a fellow had to put up with these days. "Even Steven," he mumbled. He saw coal cars heading back from the dungeons of the earth, he watched the slag piles glow and burn low, and walked out of town to find another anything but his own. He

woke to a nightmare of missed
connections and all the seats ripped up
with knives, a suicide down in
compartment 2B, a ticket punched a
trip denied.

25_____

Here's another castoff character a
veteran of the torpid zone, he gladly
interferes with the mental swamp fill
to elucidate extensively on his
abrogation of hermit intake, his hand
of one too many fingers sloping in
dormant surprise as he describes the
function of ganglia and his own
sodden method of defloration, only
pausing with that drooling leer to hold
forth on the symbiotic effect of
negating symbols, it being a bit
obvious but he's been running the
same riff for years seems he took a
patent out on his tape loop at the turn
of the millennium and was merely
protecting his alien rights.

This inventor of lugubrious sex drugs
came strolling by with hoarse promises
of eternal gratitude hurled at the pack
as they left the gate, staring at the
ceiling ripping pages off calendars
before the year was up, making
intimations he knew us when the rug
got pulled. His gray eminence dared to

charge admission to his self sacrifice, an elongated ceremony that had us all basking in the desert sun, a pale mirror hooked up to an amplifier that gave a half-assed aspect to any notion of order. Nobody's solace left him in contempt of his conductive requisition, sequestered in the mail chute with his blasphemy and orations about some fatal conspiracy, all hollow notions, inconsequential posters pasted on the subway wall, heeding not the none too subtle hints that it was time to burn the ID papers and reveal that native exterior. Slick vestige from the wrong side of Martian kicks, he scanned the street in a flashbulb instant, a trick he learned on the last reconnoiter, and masked the inert impulse to peek when the fuzz hit the cortex, bringing us all down by lashing his neophytes to telephone pole crucifixions, that basic intrusion, those shuttering breaths, that box car bootleg. He sat down in that desert of his solitude and declared civil disobedience but was unclear as to his cause and not a cop for fifty miles. He

was on the testing range anyway and
we waved goodbye as a bubbling sun
shoved naked cliffs through spectrum
changes. The biggest meteor shower of
the century found our lad skating on
the glassy sand and watching owls
wing through the ghostly spires,
humming antiquity's mellow chant,
cheerfully dividing up the land among
jackrabbit peasants and scorpion kings.

Giving everyone a fair shake he
applied for admission to the United
Nations but was denied out of hand
who do you control is all they wanted
to know. Rejected but not dejected the
land baron on his barren land
unleashed his tarantula constituency
and now we're all making contingency
plans for submarine existence,
bartering suffering souls for a piece of
the scorched earth.

26

Pythagoras the gregarious Athenian
shunted normal procedures aside and
knelt behind the columnar marble
quarry, ice cold and blue in the ninth
circle he raised his eyebrows in
expectant nervousness, sliding with
tennis shoes through the shredded
glass on his way to the humility class,
dealing yesterday's pock marked news
to adolescent leather and steel
components, hoping for one last
chance at petty revelations peaking on
the bad acid when the cops paid him a
late night surprise. His Grecian ways
fell harmless on dull ears but he
pressed on with throaty exhortations to
the nameless crowd, taking the last
train out of town with his familiar, a
crow he called little Willy, the leading
man in nobody's unwritten play.

His eyes glazed nebulous on curious
clouds hanging low over blazing acre
wide used car lots, moonless night auto
shootouts interrupting the pleasant
evening air. Sipping slowly from the

bottle without a name, hub caps spun from flashing box car transports, riding the blinds and spending time with penny-ante poker faced outlaws, hurling indelible insults at nostalgic violence, lying back in filthy exhaustion, thumb pulled out of joint and swelling by the minute, but hanging in there like we like our ancients to do. His grizzled mug smiled into cracked mirrors behind alley necklace hangovers, and into his mind flashed a remembrance of the portentous days of youth, when broken promises squatted among last night's stale hybrids.

The boy whose toes are always tapping slipped elusively through the barricades, his smiling story told with prideful performance, running his broken knuckle hand through seaweed hair, donning the embryonic derby, putting it endlessly plain, wrinkling his brow in our mirror's shoddy stare, the Latin Quarter at dawn peeling red shutters opened for the coming typhoon, to say the least erratic behavior in his portable dreary forecasts.

He was the easy street kid hitting the skids the third time around, pounding everyone on the back assuring us it was the last go round, his diving board bank account tapped from lack of interest. "I have a thing with the teller," he tells us," she tells me where the alarm button is and after we rip the joint off we'll murder each other over an argument about what color we should paint the palace walls. Hers is an infinite abundance of insular nightmares played on some morbid machine, dry lips puckering for the apple's juicy bite, a casual wave from the back booth, went cross eyed staring down my madness that night we got the pills confused. Having wrestled extensively more gruesome demons in my time I laughed the dumb hick off my reflection.

"My favorite book is the road atlas, I read it on the subway that all night ride, going through Southern towns the nadir of frontal stimulation where we got lost and drove down main street three times an old guy on the post office steps waved each time perhaps he had forgotten we had already done that route, maybe it was that bogey weed but every turn ended us up at the War Memorial.

"We had a piece of cardboard in front of the radiator and shutting off the motor meant a three hour delay and we hocked every negotiable item for gas to keep us moving, the frozen speed freak expatriate looking to add us to his jolly crew, his minions stroking their arms looking for a fresh vein, big brown eyes and flowing hair apologizing she can't take me home her husband having a bad taste in his mouth from the last American to come through town. She drove and whispered in my ear weren't we lovers in Quebec's ancient ruins, so we

headed in the opposite direction and
waited for drunken farmers to unlock
their barns so that we could shack up
in wordless passion, tripping the waiter
with his tray full of Zombies, finally
picking a pocket for a key passed out
on the large oaken table, we slashed
our tires and stuck out our thumbs
breathing a bit easier with every step
that got us away from there, until the
whole joint faded on the horizon and
we spent the night in some hostile little
border town that glowed in the
receding mist, long tracks ending in
some freight depot the silo crumbling
against the night sky, the tracks
stretching across diminishing plains.

"She got a job as a custard girl in that
little town and smiled at me shyly
behind the glass partition, fingers
aware but not touching separated by
that glass, making plans for mutual
escape, but my ragged sleeplessness
put me on the edge of town and fell out
among the milk cartons and splintered
glass, awoke to a pitiless flashlight

kicking my blistered foot edging me on to tomorrow. A dream or the real thing who can tell nowadays so I took that soft ride and awoke in Provo where the atmosphere was thin and operators mishandled her number, the little green switch and a friendly earthquake, a fit of arrogant logic, iron arabesque gates electrified against those shifting their seasons, some wise guy christening hero sandwiches and sending them off to war, a fifth columnist having pissed all over the gunpowder causing the ugly smell.

"It gets awfully cold out here at night so how about a soft ride until tomorrow? The tour bus pauses in the riot zone, shutters clicking but shaded eyes, until some clown slashed the tires and the *turista* were subject to all sorts of humiliating native rights, the witch doctor picking his teeth with that souvenir Bowie knife from the Alamo, wondering what to do with all those transistor radios. Not a crumb left in the cupboard, the lifeboat sinking having sprung a leak after insertion of a can opener from sardine frogmen, the aqualung empty due to helium hyperventilation. I stole a ride from the old man of the sea and rode down south on a banana boat filled with tarantulas out of Costa Rican registry, the captain given to epileptic fits whenever a storm brewed up, the first mate running around making gurgling sounds tying all the shorelines into nooses. Aground we went and aground I stay, here in this fickle morass."

27_____

The scholar came next his numbing
tactical combinations suggesting
confinement in verbal abuse, though it
must be said he's convivial enough for
someone who has bypassed
contemptible mind rot for his theory of
static mathematics. He slumps out of
his headquarters, a blasted rock
pounded by surly tides, his Wet
Clothes Quarterly and Dial Venus back
issues scattered on the sandy shore, a
leaking barrel filled with broken
pencils obscuring a full view of the
horizon, he's taken to wearing some
cast off leotards and a Harvard sweat
shirt his cracked sunglasses with bent
rim and the inevitable hood that
obscures hearing and his face from
curious onlookers. He's always busy
hatching innumerable plots for
invasion of privacy and assigning bait
fish ministries in the new regime,
compiling his encyclopedia of working
class rhetoric and cleavage hang-ups,
assuring all that his maps of the new
sector did not confuse the brides of

blood with the silver diner and the all night funeral parlor.

His eyes could you see them through his *optica obscura* were rear view mirrors that described the road less traveled through orange and purples neon blazing in dusty rain puddles and oil slicked streets where ornate hamburger stands fought for the view with chapels of sweet true love and his motto of course: "When you're hungry you'll eat anything."

His reminiscence of love that girl Shirl with the natural curl who left her last long lost love turning blue in a shadow green corridor under some smoky coal yard moon she packed a quick suitcase and stepped over that bundled up drifter into the soot of endless rail yards and followed the lines of electric infinity to some northern shore where she found her future ex-room mate shrinking her clothes and beckoning her to spend empty nights of cheap thrills with the consumptive scared child in the next building. She hid her eyes from the bright morning light and parted the curtain to stare at the adjacent brick wall, looked down into snow covered garbage strewn alley and paused: "Not for me to be an ancient librarian of down journals and some madman's week old socks (the scholar, we think) filing his despair in the pillbox cabinet, not for me desolate mornings cold coffee locks on the common refrigerator door, not for me fading eyes and hard rouge, not for me broken back hard core old folks home fire in the cripple ward, I've got to go away or go all the way, and this knot in my stomach still tightening." And on the way down saw the blonde child from the south walking through her first snow covered field.

But music was his great love and like a trumpeter pausing over a questionable note he flourished his claim to have archived the largest extant collection of dirty pictures academic purposes only of course and wetted his sloping

fingers as he turned each page, his
diary of temporality his life's work, his
faded pages now a placemat under
today's sad soup. His metronome
droned down the bare hallway it
echoed back his empty eyes his broken
glasses now on the linoleum floor, his
obstacles to his work just another
flimsy excuse, his afternoons spent
sleeping his terror of missing opening
night, another blown chance, another
regrettable utterance, so out go the
lights the shade is drawn back into his
hovel where his dream lover comes to
him and soothes his weary brow with
tears from a forgotten world. Then off
he goes to beat the rap smuggled in the
rear of some old station wagon old
blankets and sacks piled to make him
inconspicuous the cops they couldn't
give a shit one less sad case to close.

28_____

That green fellow approaching paid no mind to this and continued his leaning toward tarpaulin manipulations, trying to get his makeshift camp set for the next big blow. His mind's eye fixed on greedy insults he was a specially trained back snapper who sold deeds to homes where even the archeologist can't find a foundation, a highway rambler who dreaded the feeling of a loosened tie, his time spent in kidney shaped cocktail lounges where your corporals argued the morality of last night's massacre, some old grouch insisting that true patriots will not shrink from the call, the TV blaring but all the stations gone off the air the broadcast just some prerecorded verbal insistence that our leader was still alive.

"I waited three hours for breakfast," our boy complained to anyone who would listen, and that means few," the nerve of those gooks, and all they had left was hundred year old buffalo they claimed was killed by Bill, the cook slitting his wrists in a frenzy of scrambled eggs, buried under rush orders for the boys handling the mine disaster. The priests ate well you'll be glad to hear but complained when the water got turned to vinegar instead of wine, so they crucified the waiter while the bishop's wife played sonata cantata in the gymnasium to an appreciative audience of giggling acolytes in high drag, snide remarks about the blood of the lamb, most unchristian behavior wouldn't you say?

"The entire seminary was engaged in the erection, a fifty five foot all weather stainless steel stroboscopic cross, but bearded anti-papists plotted to blow it up and the boys in the oval office scratched their hairy asses trying to figure out how to stop the whole commotion. So they surrounded the joint with buses and charged everyone with anything they could think of and then shoved them aboard, no transfers allowed, and drove them out to the swamps waving flags a most glorious display, but I stood there weeping as the buses sank in the mud, everybody aboard arguing about who should sit with whom and would time tell our real story?

"I was the first one and last one out of town and I doubted that I could carry the message, so I skipped onto the last freight north wiping my brow at the close call and ordering another tall cool one as the Metroliner sped through the murky flats, spitting autos and small arms fire disrupting my train of thought, the usual professor always willing to argue some obscure notion telling me that our lives were nothing but a smaller manifestation of some unattainable godliness within us all, somewhere."

29 _____

So we're fishing in dead waters our
line snagged somebody's boots
causing the massive tug, an illusion of
activity something to do awaiting the
hurricane the shutters gone in a blink
of an eye. But lo here's another
familiar face, the Golden Boy we call
him he always shows up at odd hours
(if you're not getting even are there
any others?) with brown paper bags
ruffled at the edges he settles in the
volcanic ash we laughingly call sand to
muddle our minds with his walking
pharmacy, his dispassionate pleas his
back brain laxatives to rattle his
faithful bag of pills in our swollen ears
brandishing a dislodged spear gun a
broken gear shift knob all the classic
symptoms. His fifty cent wine head
swims in the early evening rooftops he
sees it all coming down, his acoustic
jive like the uptown swami he paid a
call he copped his plea he sat with the
faithful minions picking the fly shit out
of the caviar. His strange tastes ripped
from some iron door his arguments

moot like the time he pinned that maniac mathematician to the floor and complained about his inability to trisect a triangle.

"Impossible," he muttered, "there's a sullen willow that sits by the gray stream and the French shall pay those insensitive bootleggers trying to liquidate their incurably frozen assets their delicate collections. I've rolled around with their empties I've been banned from every bar from Bar Beach to Brighton, I've cast my eyes on misrepresented contracts I've worn the lumpen jacket festooned with antiquated condiments I've been perseverant in obnoxious causes and enough is too much. I've copped my last plea and dropped my last dime and it's bad news in anybody's book and you all need cooling. I've contemplated Drano like some fixative Bromo so do me I'm in the ovens. There's a swarm of red hot bees tickling my spine and my only need is emptiness a thousand times greater than getting in from the cold, lust hunger, just emptiness."

There was no consoling him and he melted on the spot and the maid swept him out with the evening's fallen roaches. He wandered through the midnight market, the light bulbs all strung in a row from dangling phone lines, the radios blaring on no channel at all, the static unkempt yet another temptation from the timeless belly of the all night consumption gang, heathen sentiments rippling down his chakras making their way toward some malicious mischief, assault with intent glazed on his burnt out eyes. Red dot flashes in the foreign panic button monolith, staring at black cat crossings, the only path he knew, yellow sulphur clouds hanging over the plains, back brain boiling medulla oblongata long gone, kindly administrative shock treatments working on the upper west side, nothing got in the way of this highway snake's own special brand of venom, his last victim left smoldering in disgraceful vulcanized apparition. His diet nothing but bad meat the mad cow brand soaked in crank case oil and half a loaf of white bread, his unappeased appetite leading him to bad habits.

His heartfelt diary left suspended in the tar pits, the triceratops reading it carefully looking for clues to identity and any soft pitch, the flame thrower in the cellar and noncommittal happenings recorded with care the foreign foggy drunken nighttimes caused by empire madness strung out on too many thousand watt light bulbs all in parallel circuitry the frozen dawn sounding resonant chords the dissonant butcher knives flashing in hour of the wolf declensions, sign posts pointing the wrong way out of town.

He left aside all biblical references, thankfully, there being too many of those strewn about these days, his glittering mosaic setting in neon bog sensations, robot humility

remembrances synchronized with
blinking yellow signs that warn of
highway quick death, that bleak
landscape all packed and ready to go.
Lethal arsonists arranged the calling
cards for the altruistic carnival while
he watched crystal rain fall on the
abandoned depot, kicking his deflated
beach ball through broken beer bottles
and cardboard dreams. Or looking
through faded curtains from bed and
dresser one night stands onto some
ersatz Times Square the hustle being
the dirty coat and the kindly passersby,
the blaring ads hardly caught his eye
his saliva test being positive for
homeless heroes the gory flare-ups the
Agent Orange the all night eyes the
purple street corners lingering on
tomorrow's tongue, the appointment in
Caracas he never kept.

So on they come a parade of some
useless cabalists sending tunes out
through the tree of life trying to make
the Tarot and the pinwheel all make
sense. The convicted souls the witness

after witness testifying to the
obnoxious harassment of loathsome
semi-financial sympathies, their
Leopold like lobes, their sacks of
Venzetti, in stark weather, fishing in
the Charles with the Boston angler, the
man sons of forgotten fathers, the surly
teens in their trench coats of black
pushing everyone to the limit. The
country hushed waiting for the verdict,
the yellow press blaring their black
and gray indictments, the DA's half
witted son, the hermetic longing on
green neon highways, the dusty back
streets the telephone poles frozen in
mud, the fog banking on telltale hearts,
the drums beating out similar
manifestations, the wanted posters in
general stores, the frigid scorpions
waiting in the boot camp with stingers
fixed and ready, they took blood
samples to see what time the ferry
would leave.

30_____

If this fails to impress you consider
other places and faces and how
stringent food intake can suffocate
those ingrates, all that barbed wire you
think they put it up for looks? The
moon a crack in the starless sky,
plying through pearly gates in gray
steel water, rusty water on tap the
walls fallen down an excellent chance
to meet the neighbors. The yellow
cellophane that passes for a window
the mattress that's seen much better
days the sweet ride of misery the
aimless robots the mangled keys of the
piano playing an odd tune, the fatal
touch the nebulous nodes, the fallen
arch and the belladonna eye. This is
nothing but a blissful vision of
nocturnal postulates, a soul with blue
sparks flying, a mind floating in the
aquarium of some forsaken waiting
room, a manifestation of hierarchies
and a point of no return. Take note as
the light dims for a moment, as eager
eyes scan the pale promises, as the

mobility becomes spurned as the
clouds race across the moon.

Short hair's just a fad it makes it easier
to jam the helmet on, a fanciful state of
disbelief. Rip those suits with a stiletto
knife, wet down the rug with kerosene,
forget about prime time, make those
appointments with Baal in the viewing
room. Scan the full chart impress the
computer geniuses go see your
grandmother. I know, I know, you
come from the castle with a message I
search your face for some clue your
silence your somnolence you offer me
the ten dollar reading for five a slow
day in the prediction business. We met
once in the back of a taxi heading for
the day old bread store, that bleak
landscape those midnights tugs hauling
the garbage to dump in the bay.

Your eyes all jelly you laugh at the
wind well at least that's some sign,
you blow into town with a silver pistol
and a fat bundle of artifacts eluding
that high speed chase after arranging to

lift hardware from unsuspecting innocent bystanders, these accounting upsets are nothing new, you understand, just a way of leafing through the body counts and pulling the plug on air compressors where spiders become trapped in their own webs so the commercial will just have to wait.

Newton was right. All amorphous sentiments lend nothing to demoralized souls, the doctor slaps it and you give it a name, the rules you'll find them as we go along, just evade the draft and keep a tight lid, in the land where nobody walks and street signs proclaim the misery. You get mail marked occupant and you haven't lived there for years, just can't help you out I'm a bit light and the electric bills are climbing, so just throw the little red switch and try to wring another piaster out of those revoked patents, the salesmen travel with business cards written in Canaanite hieroglyphics the scientists doing

battle for grants to study nerve gas the
library card lost somewhere in some
faded green envelope.

So pack your lunch and hit the road
and work out those neurotic impulses
to emulate your marginal lineage, be a
guard of the old school, sit in the garret
with a carrot reading Marat adjusting
your cravat, be that dusty old soul in a
stand of pine, flash on sunbeams
highlighting the cycle of birth and
death, ride the wheel and deal in
prestigious doubt, join up with the
crowd that measures a man by how
much he's suffered.

31_____

Those deadly nightshades, the Spartan
Debs, the warlords wielding spear
guns, those gray personages that slip
through unspoken alleys that finally
lay sideways on the ledge feeling the
inevitable cold stone the marble
epitaphs the carnage trade entrance the
collapsing caress, the mute line
waiting for office hours to commence.
Staring self-consciously into the gray
exhaust rolling down the boulevard,
that creaking edifice to
pharmacological vice meanders
through the garbage-strewn square to a
long hallway lit by a blinking
fluorescent light. The doctor staggers
in clutching his worn black case, his
balding head nodding to no one in
particular, his toe tapping out some
random tempo marked by slamming
doors and screaming brakes, he seems
to give casual recognition to the
booster line forming outside his steel
reinforced door.

"I keep the lads waiting like a proper Man, I ease my eye through the keyhole to spy on their despair, I beckon the first lucky inmate with calloused finger into my musty cave, the lad rolling up his sleeve as he comes through the door, I motion for him to sit in the lumpy waiting room chair. Instant energy all the classic symptoms, he feigns empathy for this conceptual madness, his graphics dealing disharmony with any view you might have of this tortured globe.

"I told him the office was open at eleven he was here at six, my chambers littered with cut up medical journals, my pins ups of lepers, my smiling betel nut chewers, my blood stained table, my dusty instruments my deft hand with the needle remember mumbly-peg? His tongue slipped and wow it hit, he scratched his kneecap *typisch* and I regarded him suspiciously when he kept eyeing my medicine cabinet, so I bade him to come down on the side room couch but

he came in occasionally to see if I was
awake and told me he wanted to soak
up the atmosphere, the gas lamps, the
leather arm chairs, the bust of
Beethoven the polka dot bow tie the
painting of some desert flower on the
edge of the Malpais.

"Those roads led past shuttering
shacks covered with hubcaps and
license plates, the songbirds leaning on
fence posts, the gulleys where no water
runs, the higher elevations with
streams like linen for the winter
wrapped, the slippery side of the bowl
of the Great Basin. Or in the badlands
where antelope kept watch from a
ridge, where midnight bats squealed on
their way to their lurid feast, where
white face cattle roam showing
nothing but white masks in the quarter
moon light.

"Those old movies, you know that
somehow through it all it becomes the
worst possible plot, those situation
tragedies, those dead eye stares, the

radio up to full volume, the crooked finger taunting me to sweet bliss on twisted sheets, fourteen cats underfed and sniffing anything that moved, the balding rug, the empty cartons filled with melted soda pop bottles some attempt at Pop art.

"The life spirit festooned in the fickle morass, the epistemology of emptiness cremated with the suicide note, elaborate solicitors pounding on the door begging to plead my case, trading broken Mesopotamian earthenware for a chance at hesitation, assassinated character references being likely in War Zone B.

"I dropped a name and my gal went off into a three week cycle of shit fits about her first love who once an up and comer thirty second man on the hip switch circuit dropped everything to devote his life's remaining breaths to find the universal symbol of suffering and dread, surfacing but twice a year at some seaside festival where salivating adolescents swinging titanium peace signs spent the night under the pier watching the moon through the slats, waves crashing against the ever-weakening pilings, the white paint long flaked, the helicopters shouting static at the roaming crowds, those cotton candy junkies, the barkers yelling at us in ancient Greek, the prize a last chance at wilted plastic flowers. Her doorknob was slippery as an eel all that body lotion and noxious perfume, ingratiating the hobos, the voters having stuck bubble gum all over the levers leaving the election in doubt.

"I watched her fade as she blazed an orange X on the arching sky, steering her leering jet toward southern plateaus, the papaya vendors fallen under their most colorful umbrellas, no doubt we'd all been on the job too long. There were machinations and soap box ravings, seen it all in sixty nine and the reruns are back again, the hip switch dealers conning the *turista*

the schematic nuances gone out of
control, those metal dog brides
vibrating in their ripped off semantics,
that verbal con nasal voice murmuring
lips indiscrete contests that revel
without a cause.

"It's easy to laugh at the heliocentric
theoreticians stumbling on their holy
logic, the defecation swami screaming
at me don't call me when I'm in my
trance it breaks my dual system. The
marketing of ephemeral links to
microboppers left my big toe tapping
on the street corner of corporate
linkages, another festering sore left
dormant under the luster of neon mud.
I left the bearded punk smiling at the
soft parade, his maturational process
having taken a recess, no vanity but
uptown excitement, all additions
lobbed off in the subdivisions of a
forlorn mind, so why not some new
river Baptism, why not a fresh start
and tenuous looks, why not the primal
scream, ten million bugs in the

billboard's harsh glare, the lobby a
vending machine dream.

"Or in my winter cave not a worthy
time all the electricity turned off
reconstructing my downfall in intricate
frenzy, no outgoing calls, the
neighbors not even curious,
threatening conviction and eviction
with every move I make. Too many
hours haunting the bleak pleasure
domes where hands reaching to touch
pause when near seemingly intangible
objects, my words fallen backwards
off stools and rolled up in the sawdust
sediment. This being the place where
the glaciers melted leaving all the crap
they'd picked up on the way south,
where ghosts who survived the plague
fixed their gaze on blizzard street
reflections and gray fog floats before
weary eyes waiting for the
appointment no one keeps, every one
so deep in the woods that their
connections meld with the coolest
center of lethargy, the spell broken

occasionally by the flare-up caused by the fact that I was there.

"Anything you got in mind is fine with me, I can see by the way your neck slides under your head and that bloody eye dangling by its thread that you are a bona fide member of our planet's liberation movement, your doctoral dissertation on misrepresentation just another dodge to keep you out of empty booths staring into the bottle's empty mouth, another space wasting corpse drifting dreary in vestigial sewage this crystal fog can't shroud the emptiness, offering cold wind and loneliness to anyone who cares to get involved. This old fish has swum upstream a thousand times and still ends up on this beach, finding myself fading fast as the night wears on, and back at the same trade entrance the next morning. So I will come back after a month of days, perhaps to find your flesh still crumpled in that dawn's frosted light, perhaps to find you under

the palms your flesh turning a duller
blue."

32_____

Pausing to see if the light would
change our refugee from the
reclamation center sat on his shotgun
shattered beer keg, more detritus from
our fulsome tide, to punctuate our
eardrums with jabs from his faded pink
swizzle stick, beckoning all the
stumblebum *turista* to rest a moment
in his accumulated garden of twisted
metal to hear his tragic story of a latent
symbol gone awry and the bust out of
bestial madness. It's all about hard
times and how little one can get by
with, what with our hovels nothing
more than rotundas of spot lit dung
heaps. Those equinox gamblers
balancing the egg surging toward the
betting window exclusion, those blister
bigots reaping filthy profits on
telephone pole crucifixions, those idiot
impulses that neon beaver above the
lumber yard all laughing in the rain
while they straddled the white line.

Our boy lifts his armless hand to signal
some confluence of heavenly jaundice,

his perpetual stagnation bubbling slowly through the hard knocks and constantly recycled coffee grounds, him beseeching all who would hear to pause for his eloquence about the midnight abyss, foul clouds rising on the invisible horizon, him letting everyone know twas' high time to reveal closet madness on the pilgrim's road to the bleeding stone.

"I remember the good old days a younger sport I be then seemingly endless heathen kicks in the back stable endurance, my control indelible my latent flesh arrayed in organic meekness, hoping for some paisley delights the pinnacle of my symbiosis flying high mythically. I engaged devices intricate through the foggy night blazing, shredding that line that separates the gesture from the word, romantic terms like the curling leech, hateful moments laughed away in sardonic wheeze, my decrepit lungs, my health a debate of my universal subject.

"I fled that momentary lapse into a
faster moon, the tides here draw
objects curious into my sea cave, those
undreamt nightmares conspiring with
the recent kidnappings to make the last
bus out of town. I of course
sympathize with the hopeless
contender, the reckless eyes burning
with the cold fire of conceptual
duplicity. Now I sit here surveying the
smoldering landscape with infinite
congestion, honoring a past fading fast
not taking any bets on tomorrow. I
confess I did my best with the burning
vest, the torments of hesitation's
screaming suffocation, that decay in
the back alley a distant relation,
pointing to the sky but never
questioning why, just have to rely on
sensitivity that sits sullen in nervous
reply, the meandering stream of my
life seen as a dream damned up with
unheralded sacrifice, like the first time
I spied our shipwreck here (yes, I was
the first to spy him) and didn't even go

through his pockets for spare organs,
just left him here peacefully to die.

"Yellow to green and blue in between,
a distant squealing marks the
impatience to oblivion, the strafing
crews flew low avoiding the bombed
out factory figuring any life stirring in
those ruins was punished enough and
didn't need any more lessons in
control's respectful suffering. My
lethal pointer savage in refutable
impositions, my leery friends, you who
sit sacrosanct in your closet, you speed
freaks objective about your concluding
demise, you bunch of numbskulls you
just sit around rehashing your
levitation memoirs. I cased out the
whole lot, but they deprive me of my
ugly denials. They force me into
perjury in the ephemeral courts, the
only noble path being obsession.

"Needless to say it kept me busy
slaughtering any trace of identity until
I picked up this echo technique and
was able to go transparent at whim's

jolly convenience. I was three basic entities substituting themselves to fit the current crime and made quite a name for myself screaming at the top of my lungs at inauspicious times, those moments of invisible tension that made everybody think that they were calm, I knew better and let it be known, them rushing at me with their tranquil mantras. I just faded back and switched them to machines, sometimes frankly amazed at their odd maneuvering, caressing numb hands with feigned kindness. I disguised myself as a tenant behind on the rent and evicted the premises, left obscure notes about my whereabouts leading them through twisted paths to inevitable dead ends. Sometimes I'll call in late night bomb scares just to keep them on their toes, turning their yellow to orange and that glorious red. My functions now brief and to the point, sequestered here on this likely throne, the phone long disconnected the drain clogged with treaties of discontent.

"So my dear shipwreck I will my circumstances to you, you being a kindly historical misnomer judging by the way your host scrapes your jugular with that rusty razor no doubt contemplating his eventual duty."

Our boy hauled himself off with his shattered throne, shuffled through the debris and made his way back to his guilty cave, smashing broken bottles and yelling, "Sleep on!"

33 _____

Our sky still with the heaviness of
unending wait, the next soul shuffles
forward (always one more) bending
backwards to repel the aversion for
licensed bondage, his tee shirt caked
with sweat and blood from ancient
battles on ploughed plains, his chords
changing yet still chiming in on that
same old tune, his ascent ruffled by the
swaggering mass, his land cleared for a
bitter crop, his semblance of self
confusing the rattle dance with some
misbegotten reaper, driving around the
bend waiting for the acid to hit.
Parched throat and mind leading him
to drink out of our tidal pools, no cure
for thirst that, wrapping himself in a
blanket against the harsh wind, the
syncopation of his turbulence
mismatched with a troubled
conscience. The librarian of causality
placed his index card in her melting
cabinet, tapping his shoulder in the
reading room and requested the elderly
code, so he just shrugged and left to

look for a shower, his confessions
ripped to confetti blowing in the wind.

"I certainly need some lounging year
on some quiet hill this heathen hunger
distributed to any lover's ambush that
smoke hanging in the air that mute
discontent that other self waving at me
from across a fleshy border. Any mild
attacks are swept away but always
wiping my brow with razor blades in
the shrapnel blizzard, those nightmare
mashed potatoes, some evil cook in the
kitchen chuckling as he sprinkles
ground glass in my feast. I pawned
everything in sight for my nasty
mobility habit and searched for the
temples of misplaced contingencies,
swiftly regretting the grin I gave the
cop, he not in the mood I was in.
There's a reckless wind blowing today
there's some red light blazing with
tenacious glare some outlaw
transformer is outputting the wrong
current an incredible likeness to the
softest touch of all.

I need some space. I need some air. I need some time. I can't do everything at once I can't make it to my own breakdown, I can't dip this meek flesh into rusty waters I can't find mirrors to see my eyes."

34_____

Some characters, like us all, just come
and go met briefly in points of transit
or noticed at the next table at a cafe
perhaps no words are exchanged but
there is always experience, observation
and of course projection where do we
get notions of familiarity? Well, here's
one:

The king of the stumblebum hall of
fame he may stagger but his infancy is
spread around the alley walls, his
keepsake toothbrush and spoon
strapped to his ankle a fail-safe method
I am told the picture in our inevitable
locket--lowly metaphor for what is
kept sacred close and private--his
beard faded on green cigar spittle bad
air and misbegotten love in a long
faded home movie where the jerky
motion is offset by the scratches in the
film caused by the rickety projector of
his mind and tears where the tension
became too great and there's no sound
only images viewed through a glass
poorly lit faded color sequences out of

sequence no context no contest a torn
moment from an imagined continuum
projected on a thin wall where the
coughs come through at night, that
veneer, that mist, that image formed by
association with myths created by
fragments of loneliness interconnected
with tenuous love.

The king's cowboy compass pointed
north a direction that would hopefully
evacuate his overheated demeanor
through plantation swamps and
lanterns swaying on the bayou breeze,
moaning cows croaking frogs in a
chorus of dull surprise echoing around
the moon with zodiac sky and gas
station sulphur lamps inviting
incredible moths to the final light up.
Sudden upstart violence lingers on his
thorazine eyes, interns running
outward for the patio prognosis, the
mews of outlaw cats playing around
his whiskers--stop the party and say
cheese--the mist around the cathedral
at night those cobblestones difficult to

navigate the upper rooms crowded the
superintendent too lenient with his
jangling keys.

The portable dehydration machine
tours the slums tonight hurry up it's
the cops do you want to go again? The
conditions were of course appalling the
streets littered with support groups
embarrassed by misrepresentation of
the times of arrival that keep shifting
like the tote board at the track, the
storm throwing off the schedule of all
those hoping for any return on
investment.

It's a definite talent to deal with the
affording of war and neglect. Time
tells tales or never ticks the clock when
the jails are active and parole is out of
control, tampering with the jury's
private parts tempering it all with the
local files. Who knows what
information has been handled by
taxable innocents? By any standard it's
a pernicious deal that deems to certify
interference with the rank and file,

those sneaky people computers that
spew unverified problems after a quick
phone call at the trial. Perjured priests
connive with smiling prosecutors on
the night of the crime in question, a
more foul than usual collusion between
evaporating three alarm fires when he
and his pals show up in kimonos and
the boy with the shovel marveled at the
bursting surprise. There was no word
on the cause of the craze, just more
sniggering civil war soda jerks.

The soulless king flapped his sole-less
shoe and threatened a weapons
buildup, akin to offering bankruptcy to
those who could least afford it. Zone
battalion shock troops were up to the
task and happy to be meat cleavers,
while the dismantled spokesman
incapable of offending all day Sunday
murmured something in the trenches
that no one heard the moment before
the manufactured lead shut his mouth.

The jury is studying maps of the
massacre site, one of them a six year

old policeman and all came to find
forty-five peaceful solutions naturally
the king swept them aside and chose
the most brutal, difficult and
dangerous he'd be observing by
satellite but of course we'd all be
praying for you, the shoe salesman on
the draft board does not weep in the
parking lot the cement floor is where
we exercise you don't see cushioned
mats on the street, do you?

The elders lit a hot foot under the card-
carrying embryo while high-life
musicians hurried through the clear
light with remembrances of electrical
detonations and the gymnast flying
through the air. The definitive sparks
backlit the palm trees where jumping
spiders watched us cavort. There were
no clues to helter skelter weapons
possession when states of confusion
reigned in the committee on age,
meager, forgotten unprotected and old
waving good-bye through mesh glass
doors, too many struggles for the
dwindling meat, foresworn promise the

wilted petunia shuttered with forgotten and empty lives.

Mashed potatoes and boiled carrots again in pre-dawn fluorescent glare, it won't get any better than this and proud of it. This is how we build character it's quite a feat. Chairs make this awful sound on linoleum. I've always hated the sound of a pushed back chair maybe it was one particular flare-up or just the tenor of the joint, the slap perhaps but if you want more coffee you get more coffee but you better know when the last lunch is given out because you'll get on line and it will move but there won't be anything left when you get to the end and no one will clue you in at least not directly just bits and pieces of a frequency that only few radios receive. The bodily demand makes very hazy forecasts and insults block the view.

The judge of the group drew up the charges, mostly to do with dramatic maladjustment and closed-circuit endeavors. His sense of balance had obviously been cast aside on a night filled with probabilities and everyone was suspect.

Like I was saying we were running down this fire escape with the armored personnel carriers on the facing street and the armed personnel hitting the bricks like some old movie and that was close the fake ermine and the exchange of addresses of course we both tore up the paper when just out of sight it was raining in the gallery of reality and there was the attempted escape. The king heard the charges read:

"Your tie is too loud, your goals are through other sources, your necessary establishments are inequitable to domestic pogroms, your pen strokes need moral persuasion and a bit more character dialog and development with the straight and narrow, your leaning back situations reveal a shameless opportunist and especially your

adversaries. There can be no
compromise with a grammar that
dislodges the physics of perception or
creases the collar of the unjustified,
that concedes nothing to describe the
energy or events that lead to white
clouds in your inane and decidedly
urban sky."

The king cringed to hear such charges
and faded that reality into his own flow
in union with a boycott on their eyes.
Of course he was guilty any joker
could see that so now to the sentence.

"You will be forced to exchange your
active index to coast on federal
mortgage pill box profits, to
systematize your insect advantages for
contracts with international dubious
return operations. Many have led the
way and you shall follow like a
sparrow in a flock aloft when the
shotgun blares and the spray of lead
plucks a few from the sky it's nothing
personal it's a flock and if some should
fall in the defense of our ways then it

is ordained and here comes the prelate again a sure sign that an even heavier wool is about to be pulled over your eyes."

The king took it well but shifted his feet and mumbled something unfriendly when requested to testify about how his mind had changed and how after bathing in the clear light of their logic and their appeal to all that was holy and patriotic he saw the way. "Misleading advertising" was all he could manage, the consequences of the utterance oblivious to the fact that they were ready to revoke his license for breathing anyway.

The court turned its back and posted a sign saying "Unnecessary noise prohibited", no horn honking in the hospital zone, where a short walk led past doctors milling about, the gate turning red in the sunset on the edge of the cliff where feet dangled and shots were fired. The court convened, more harsh eye glut as dawn spread its frosty

fingers down the legs of the farmer
whose toes tingled with that first taste
of gangrene.

The king's streak ends with one last
foot over the fence in the back yard,
only the remnants of the Sunday
edition blowing twisted down the
alley, in dreams, where for him there is
no awakening, only going back, page
by page, until the circle is complete.

35_____

The last message is for you my friend
the eyes that have driven these roads
the hopes of all those suffering
moments the delays in transit caused
by some mix-up down the line. The
last entry is a garbled message a thin
smile that it's all been happenstance,
an endless trap some flickering syntax
some dreary combinations assembled
for a hybrid mix. As we fade to black
we superimpose our shipwreck on the
credits, holding him aloft like those
broken spires, and we'll send it down
to rewrite for a quick chop job and
ease on back to our cave. Got the
headphones on now the only thing
coming in is direct input straight
between the ears, waiting for the
spider's head to move, reeling in the
faces of the ancient cafeteria, waiting
with swollen ears for the noise to be
words once again, all leading to total
lack of comprehension in the final
analysis.

Addendum

Our shipwreck stirs and yearns to tell
you a tale of his own, his bragging
about conquests of those lateral
transitions, sipping that numb tea in
the umbrage zone, heaping some
scrawl to further deface these pages,
those crystal reflections that dance hall
jive. Crazy as a loon and threatening to
prove it, like getting paranoid when the
spaghetti begins to move, those urban
temptations those terminal
juxtapositions those pleas for
compassion gone unheard. I pause here
on the momentary abyss; I cede the
floor, shedding my skin nice to be
naked again.

"Lights glazed off mirrors swathed in
crystal beads, each facet another face
the dance floor dense with all the
bodies in darkness, the one face
glowing softly rocking gently hands
too jagged for one so young. At the bar
a crush arms reaching out the temple
deities in the tin roofed sections of the
city where rain falls with a crackle and

steaming puddles mark the floor. My hands sought that hardness that I knew sat under her veneer, those eyes red the way the skin fled from her mouth all virgin clay ready for the potter's caress. Perhaps those cheeks could be shaped to a more expressive mold perhaps that brow could be more furrowed.

"My hand slipped and knocked over the glass and I pushed back from the table and then spun around, that's when the strobe caught me. My eyes went all white then red and then the inevitable blue dot lingered and bounced with my head. What white-jacketed man is slipping something into his case? The ice yielded to the soiled cloth. A metallic dress one strap dangling that face smeared with lipstick and rouge tongue pushed into cheek and arms oddly akimbo. With that, a hand touching an ear a secret hello? Eyes startled but pleasantly so, somehow bothered by the accompanying tableau, the tablecloth

all shoved together the strewn candles
still burning the dismembered bouquet.
A profile at the base of an inverted
triangle the face jutting up as if
overhearing words it feared to hear,
eyes wandering in deep sockets, left
arm reaching out but the hand
obscured by a dark cloth. Then all
faces gone soft bodies shifted again
and the point of focus that night there
were only planes of focus no depth
perhaps it was the darkness.

"Three figures assembled themselves
the one in front tilting his head
questioningly an unlit cigarette resting
on his lips yet he seemed indifferent to
a match, his arms folded grasping his
elbows a red light careening of his ear
an angular cheekbone the remainder of
his features shrouded in blue, those
reciprocal shadows perhaps or just the
ambient light. The other silhouetted by
a window that threw yellow light his
hand perched on the table curled like a
spider about to leap his head jutting
forward in a caricature pf

attentiveness, as if the implications of thought had been tossed aside. The last looked away, elbow on table chin flat on palm, him being in green, yet the yellow light spilled over his shoulders and rimmed the neck of the bottle before him.

"From nowhere a voice: They wait along the tracks until the trains laden with fruit disrupt their slumber, or along the river and awake when the tide caresses their sheets, silence stalks their demeanor their ancient hunger knows no peace. They peer through the glass caked with dust and the particles render them well almost painterly, and they stare into your world with the same wonder with which you consider theirs, their faces pressed closer to the glass while yours recoils into the darkness of your chamber.

"My eyes scan the ceiling my head tilted back, an escalator with silver ribbons for handrails, and another assault of the flash struck my eyes.

One said you are welcome to drink but perhaps you might have better fortune in the marketplace, the exit an archway of white stucco, the waxed wooden door studded with antique brass, the light etching a pathway out of the alley, the air like an open oven the dogs lying in shadow. Lacking knowledge of the city (I am accustomed to taxis not the common transport) I made my way through the bazaar, where leathery hands grasped reed baskets filled with squirming frogs. The figure bent to life a green hose and sprayed the amphibians so they would not explode in the relentless sun. The junks lay in the harbor tied together a gangplank between them children with shirts but no pants squatted in the filth dismembering live crabs. A shop window gave no clues, an antiquarian's stall filled with masks, carefully carved wood resembling the grimace that spoke of the wearer's future pain. An open square revealed rows of cages from which dyed birds struggled to escape, an alley again with shafts of light playing through the grating where the brown shoulders of youth already hunched bent under sacks with millet that spewed endlessly from a grinding wheel pulled by dazed donkeys.

"There were others and they walked in circles, living off the scraps of the market, the random fruit that fell from the trains, the dead fish that washed in with the tide, they sit on the high stones near the fountain. They saw me sitting in that chair, my head thrown back my exit from that bar my wandering through the alleys my loss of consciousness on that ship the swirling storm the wreck upon the coral my ears filled with the tales of these desperate souls.
All, all were glad to hear this tale, as it spoke of blood coursing through veins, of eyes that once saw although some nasty habits hinted at in the diatribe might foul the stew. But I in my eventual duty am bound to supply for

that pot, am lashed to this shore awaiting the spoils of the inevitable storm. It is my duty, my calling and may I venture to say my fate to end this take with a dull razor and a quick thrust. Those before you were jurors and you yourself be the judge, it is now time to make some dinner with this sinner and wait for the next ship to collide. Adieu!